"You don't know a thing about it!"

Christina spoke in anger and disappointment, but Duert answered her smoothly.

"Oh, but I do. I was standing at my window yesterday when you saw Adam leaving with that woman." He added with curious intentness, "And why should you be so sure he doesn't love you just because he was taking out a girl he has known for years?"

Christina smiled sadly. "He told me he was going back on duty. He lied." She said, suddenly fierce, "Oh, why can't you just leave me alone? How could you possibly understand? You don't know what it is to love someone!"

He gave her a quick look from under half-shut lids. "I'm sorry you think that," he said, "but I won't say any more about it now." His words seemed loaded with meaning Christina couldn't understand....

Betty Neels spent her childhood and youth in Devonshire before training as a nurse and midwife. She was an army nursing sister during the war, married a Dutchman and subsequently lived in Holland for fourteen years. She now lives with her husband in Dorset, and has a daughter and grandson. Her interests are reading, animals, old buildings and writing. On retirement from nursing, Betty started to write, incited by a lady in a library bemoaning the lack of romance novels.

THE BEST *of*

BETTY NEELS

NOT ONCE BUT TWICE

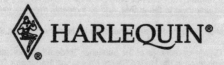

HARLEQUIN®

TORONTO • NEW YORK • LONDON
AMSTERDAM • PARIS • SYDNEY • HAMBURG
STOCKHOLM • ATHENS • TOKYO • MILAN • MADRID
PRAGUE • WARSAW • BUDAPEST • AUCKLAND

ISBN 0-373-51146-9

NOT ONCE BUT TWICE

First North American Publication 2001.

Copyright © 1981 by Betty Neels.

This edition published by arrangement with Harlequin Books S.A.

® and TM are trademarks of the publisher. Trademarks indicated with
® are registered in the United States Patent and Trademark Office, the
Canadian Trade Marks Office and in other countries.

Visit us at www.eHarlequin.com

Printed in U.S.A.

CHAPTER ONE

IT HAD BEEN raining heavily from a leaden sky, so
that the late September afternoon was already set-
tling into an early dusk. People were hurrying
home from work, their faces for the most part ill-
tempered, for the morning had been fine and um-
brellas had seemed unnecessary. The bus queues
were long, impatient to get home; surging to and
fro to avoid the fine sprays of dirty water thrown
up by the traffic. The girl who joined the queue
outside St Athud's Hospital sighed gently; if she
hadn't been so late off duty, she would have
missed the evening rush hour and been home by
now; as it was the shops were already shut and she
would have to change her plans for the evening
meal. She frowned a little, debating the advantages
of sausages over macaroni cheese. Sausages were
quick of course…a sharp prod in her back reminded her that the queue was moving, but there
were so many people ahead of her she had little
chance of getting on the bus. Indeed, she was at
the steps when the conductor came rattling down
the stairs, bellowing 'Full up!' and rang the bell.
At the same time he saw her and swung her on
board just as the bus pulled out.

'Cor, Sister, almost left yer be'ind,' he declared cheerfully. 'Yer should 'ave shouted...'

She smiled at him and shook her head. 'That was nice of you, Mr Collins. How's the chest?'

He handed out a few tickets before he answered her and she listened gravely, her fine grey eyes on his cheerful face. They were quite beautiful eyes, heavily fringed with curling dark lashes, redeeming an ordinary face from plainness, for her mouth, though sweetly curved, was too wide and her nose tiptilted, and her light brown hair was drawn back too severely from her face, although the damp air had allowed one or two curling tendrils to escape. But the conductor could see no fault in her. When he had been stricken with asthma, unable to breathe and scared to death, it had been she who had been ready with the ephedrine when the wheezing started, and if it grew worse, the aminophyline injections, and she who had calmed him down, assured him that he wasn't going to die, restored his cheerful Cockney humour. He thought of her as an angel and good looks didn't come into it.

He went on down the bus presently, leaving her standing crushed against the door with an over-large woman flattening her on the other side, a circumstance so common to her that she hardly noticed. She was a serene young woman with plenty of common sense and while not quite content with her lot, prepared to accept it—indeed, she had reminded herself on several occasions, she hadn't much choice. She was twenty-seven, and while not exactly unkissed, certainly unwed and as far as she could see, likely to remain so.

Her journey was a short one. She got off at a busy junction and turned into a road of mid-Victorian houses, their uniformity broken here and there by a shop and occasionally by a small block of modern flats. It was a depressing road, still respectable and reasonably quiet, but she had never quite got used to it. At the end of the second terrace of houses there was a crossroads and she turned into the left-hand road, to stop a few doors down before a house which was rather better maintained than its neighbours and whose door bore a brass plate with 'Doctor G. H. Forbes' engraved upon it. It was still ajar, for although evening surgery was over the receptionist would be tidying up and getting things ready for the morning. The bleak little lobby opened on to a narrow hall carpeted in a useful brown and brightly lighted, showing a door on either side, shut, and one at the end, half open. She shut the door behind her and her brother's voice called: 'Christina, I'm in the study.'

She went to the half-open door and into the room beyond, a small room, its walls lined with books, two elderly chairs by the empty fireplace, and a desk in one corner. Her brother was sitting behind it, a serious-looking man in his thirties, bearing the good looks which had passed his sister by. He smiled at her as she came in and she saw then that there was someone with him; a young man sitting easily in one of the chairs. He got up as she stood looking at him and smiled at her, and she, usually so calm and sensible, felt her heart lurch and thunder against her ribs. Here was the man, she told herself wildly, the one she'd been waiting for, tall and slim, with the kind of good looks one imagined and never saw... His eyes were the bluest she had ever seen and his hair, very dark, curled elegantly over his collar. She became aware that her mouth was a little open, so she closed it with a rush and smiled back at them both, once more her sensible self.

'I'm late,' she offered, 'sorry about that,' and waited to be introduced.

'This is Adam ter Brandt, he's over here to do a short course of anaesthetics—we met in Brussels last year at that seminar.' And as she held out a hand: 'Adam, this is Christina, my sister—she's Medical Ward Sister at St Athud's, and she house-keeps for me.' As he spoke Christina noticed a strange expression cross his face and wondered what it was. She must remember to find out later; George Henry was worried about something and she wondered what, but only for a second. Their visitor was speaking, asking her questions about

her work in fluent accented English, looking at her
with an obvious admiration which quite threatened
to take her breath.

Presently she said: 'How about coffee? It won't
take a minute.' At the door she asked: 'Supper, too,
if you care to stay? Nothing exciting—macaroni
cheese—the shops were shut.'

The coffee was accepted but supper declined on
the grounds of a prior engagement. And if I'd been
offered macaroni cheese, I'd have had a prior engagement too, thought Christina, getting coffee in
the kitchen behind the stairs, and she fell to wondering about their visitor. He looked a lot younger
than George Henry; probably younger than herself.
She paused in measuring out the coffee to take a
quick look in the small mirror over the wall cupboard. She looked every day of her twenty-seven
years, in no time at all she'd have wrinkles and
grey hairs. There wasn't time to have a good look
now, but she would when she went to bed—there
was that wildly expensive cream one of the older
Sisters had been talking about, guaranteed to hold
back the advancing years... But at least she was
slim, although she could have wished to have been
a little taller.

She made the coffee and carried it back to the
study where she sat down and poured it out with
a serenity she was far from feeling.

Adam ter Brandt went shortly afterwards, and

because George Henry plainly had work to do at his desk, Christina collected up the coffee cups and went into the kitchen to get their supper. The receptionist had gone by now and the house was quiet as she started her cooking. With it safely in the oven she went upstairs to her room, tidied herself and then sat down before the dressing table again, to take down her hair once more and pin it in a different style so that the little curls had a chance to show themselves and she looked—she hoped—younger. She told her reflection that she was being silly as she did it, but all the same she left it like that and went on sitting, suddenly faintly discontented. The room, she decided, glancing round her, was nice enough, but it wasn't pretty. When she had first come to live with George Henry, he had already furnished the house and in the three years she had been with him she hadn't liked to change anything; it was his, and although she was his sister, she had no right to alter his home.

She had been glad at the time to join forces with him. Their mother had died so very soon after their father, leaving Christina lonely in the small Somerset cottage. She had been nursing in the nearby town then, going home very often, not bothering overmuch about the future, but left on her own there had been no point in staying there—besides, she had discovered that the house and most of the small amount of money which had been left had gone to George Henry. It had shocked her when he had told her that he was going to sell it, although she could quite see the sense in that; a young GP, just setting up on his own, needed money behind him. She had never let him see how much she had minded leaving the country, but had fallen in with his idea of getting a job in London and sharing his house. She had found a good job, too; going to and fro hadn't been all that difficult, there was a splendid little woman who came in to clean three times a week and she supposed that in time, if she really tried, she would get to like London; the London they lived in—in a road like thousands of other roads, where no one knew anyone else and all the houses looked alike. The birds couldn't be heard above the traffic and there wasn't much sky to be seen.

She had gone back to Somerset several times to stay with friends, not trusting herself to look at her old home, hating to come back, but she had said nothing to George Henry. He was content with his work, determined to get on and buy another practice in a better part of London, but only when he was ready for it. He was a good doctor and worked hard and he was a kind brother. At least she had someone.

She went downstairs and took a look at the macaroni cheese, then went into the dining room to lay the table. It was a small rather gloomy room and furnished in the modern style which Christina didn't really care for; she liked old pieces, not necessarily matching each other, and bits and pieces of china and silver lying around. Of course, she reminded herself loyally, that would never do for George Henry, for Mrs Tate wouldn't have the time to dust them. The sitting room led out of the dining room and always reminded her forcibly of a show window in a furniture shop; modern again and quite uncluttered. She wandered in and out of it again, not quite knowing why, her head regrettably full of Adam ter Brandt. It seemed a great pity that having actually met a man to stir her well-balanced heart, she should be forced to lose sight of him immediately.

She laid the table in a careless fashion and, reminded of supper by a strong whiff of cheese, went to the kitchen again.

George Henry wasn't working when she went to call him to his meal, just sitting staring in front of him, but when she asked if there was something the matter, he assured her that there wasn't, ate a hearty supper while he regaled her with his day's work, and then excused himself with the plea that he still had some notes to write up. 'So I'll say goodnight, Christina,' he finished as he hurried from the room—almost, she thought, as though he were avoiding her.

They met at breakfast, but only briefly—it was far too early in the morning to talk. She had to leave the house at a quarter to eight, and he had his surgery at half past eight. Christina cleared the table with speed, left the dishes piled up for Mrs Tate and left the house. It was a splendid autumn morning. She looked at the drab road and thought of the glowing trees and the wisps of smoke from bonfires and the hedges full of sloes and the cottage she still missed so abominably. In a few years, perhaps, when George Henry was well and truly established, they would buy a little house and spend their weekends there. He showed no signs of wanting to marry; she had asked him that so often and he had laughed and told her that he wasn't the marrying kind and weren't they perfectly content to stay as they were? And until now she had been. She quickened her pace towards the bus stop, telling herself sharply that it was ridiculous to allow a brief meeting with someone to unsettle her well ordered life.

Once at the hospital there was little chance of daydreaming. The changing room, a small dark room hidden away under the stairs which led up to the Medical Wards, was already occupied by Beryl Frith, the Women's Medical Ward Sister, and two part-time staff nurses who worked for her. They all exchanged brief good mornings and got on with the difficult business of putting on caps and getting into uniforms in as small a space as possible. Christina, sliding out of a jersey dress and into a navy blue cotton one, listened with half an ear to the other girls' gossip, while she mentally reviewed the day ahead of her. Nurse Trent had a day off, and one of the student nurses had a lecture at ten o'clock and it was Dr Robinson's round; they'd have to scuttle round to be ready by eleven o'clock... Her thoughts were interrupted by Beryl, who had been talking to her and hadn't got an answer.

'What I said was,' she repeated patiently, 'Freddy took me to that new restaurant in Greek Street last night—heavenly food, though I'm not sure what I was eating not that it mattered,' she went on dreamily, 'with Freddy there. You ought to try it some time, Chrissy.'

'It sounds great,' Christina agreed cheerfully. 'I must find someone to take me.' She bent to see into the tiny mirror and arrange her cap, and Beryl gave her a quick look. Chrissy was such a dear, always so calm and self-possessed and good-tempered a touch too matter-of-fact, though. And so capable and practical. Men liked a girl to be a bit helpless about things like unblocking sinks and changing electrical plugs and not knowing which bus to catch, but Chrissy could do all those things without fuss, taking them for granted in the nicest, most unassuming way, which probably was why the few men of her acquaintance, while liking her, tended to ask her advice and then go out with some feather-witted blonde.

Christina made her way upstairs to the top floor of the medical wing, exactly on time as she always was. During her training she had suffered long waits to go off duty in the morning because the Ward Sister had been late, and she had vowed then that if ever she became a Ward Sister she would make a point of arriving on the dot.

The two night nurses were waiting for her now, pale and heavy-eyed from eleven hours of duty. Christina bade them good morning, sat down composedly at her desk and listened to the night report without interruption. At the end of it she made one or two necessary comments, made a note or two and sent them off duty before her day staff nurse, Carole Pring, put her head round the door and was bidden to come in. Carole did so, bearing two mugs of tea and shutting the door neatly behind her with a foot.

'That new man, Sister,' she began at once, 'his BP's too low. Would you take a look presently? And young Tate is complaining about his head again.'

Christina cast her eyes over the report once more. 'Ah yes—the night staff mention it too. I'll get Dr Fisher to have a look before Dr Robinson comes—he can take a look at Mr Truscott too.

We'll alter his observations to half-hourly, don't you think?' She took a sip of tea. 'They're getting the patients ready for X-ray? Good, and there's Mr Soames's barium swallow at half past nine. You take Nurse Bates with you until she goes to lecture; the other two can make beds and get people up, that leaves Mrs Toms to take patients down to the departments.' She swallowed the rest of her tea while she sorted the post on her desk. 'I'll do my round.' She smiled at the girl opposite her, her grey eyes twinkling. 'Oh, and you'd better take Mr Soames down, Carole—Ken's on duty this morning.'

Carole blushed and giggled. She was twenty-one and pretty and she and the assistant radiographer spent all their free time together. 'I say, thanks awfully, Sister!' She added happily: 'He's taking me to see *Private Lives* this evening.'

Christina watched her go: that was twice in less than half an hour—first Beryl with her Freddy, and now Carole with Ken. She didn't know that she sighed as she got up and went into the ward.

It was a long ward of twenty-eight beds, not yet modernised, so that the beds faced each other in rows against the walls. There were two side rooms too where the very ill were nursed or occasionally a private patient, although they had a wing of their own in the centre block.

Christina went into the first of these now, to greet the old man sitting up in bed, glasses askew on his beak of a nose, reading *The Times*. He looked up as she went in and without saying good morning began a forceful summing up of what the government should do immediately. Christina listened quietly, her intelligent face very calm while she looked him over. He had been in hospital for more than a week with cardiac asthma and wasn't improving. It was a pity that he had no family to bother about him; his wife had died years ago and his two sons were both abroad and not in the least interested. She had tried once to get him transferred to the Private Wing, but he had objected so strongly that she had given it up; she supposed she would have him for a very long time, giving extra work to her nurses, wanting things they hadn't got, demanding attention while he read out long articles from *The Times* when there were a thousand and one jobs waiting to be done...

'I expect you're right,' she commented. 'These people can be so exasperating, can't they? Here are several letters for you, I daresay they'll make pleasanter reading.' She added: 'How do you feel today?'

'Not bad—couldn't sleep, though.'

She nodded. 'I'll get your pills changed. You shall have a good night tonight, Colonel.' She smiled and slipped from the room and into the next one. The young man with the headache was there. She saw that he looked ill and strained and when she spoke to him he answered drowsily. Not so good, she decided; the sooner Dr Fisher saw him the better. His pulse was too slow and although he hadn't been vomiting since his admission less than two days ago, she was prepared to bet her month's money on a cerebral tumour. He was due for X-ray that morning, but he wasn't fit to move. He'd been admitted for observation and it had been decided to give him a day's bed rest before starting on a number of tests, and although she had suggested an X-ray when he was admitted, Dr Fisher, who knew everything, had told her importantly that rest was far more important. Well, he had better think again, she thought as she whipped back into the office and asked the lodge to get him urgently.

He was inclined to be ill-tempered when he turned up ten minutes later. He had been up several times during the night and after a far too brief nap was about to sit down to a hearty breakfast, and instead of that here he was facing a calm-eyed young woman, telling him without heat to do something quickly. 'And I do mean quickly,' said Christina, not losing one ounce of her habitual serenity. 'Dr Robinson will be here at eleven o'clock and if he finds Mr Tate like this heaven knows what he'll do to you.' She urged him towards the bed, saying softly: 'It's just my guess, but do you suppose it could be a cerebral tumour?'

John Fisher didn't much like Christina. He re-

spected her judgment, admired her cool which she
never seemed to lose, and agreed with everyone
else that she was a thoroughly splendid nurse as
well as a loyal friend; perhaps it was because of
these that he adopted a cocksure attitude towards
her and why he said now: 'I've thought that all
along. Get him to X-Ray at once, will you, and let
me have his notes.'

She did both, forbearing to mention that beyond
the bare fact of Mr Tate's admission there was pre-
cious little else written up. When she came back
presently from seeing the patient safely to X-Ray,
it was to find that Dr Fisher had filled a page with
meticulous observations and added a query cerebral tumour at the end.

She finished her round after that before getting
down to the task of having the ward ready for Dr
Robinson, who had a fiend's temper concealed behind his urbane appearance. But the round went
off very well. Dr Robinson had most of the beds
and behaved rather as though he had all of them,
making a kind of royal progress down the ward.
But nothing could fault his manner towards his patients; he was pleasant, reassuring and listened patiently while they talked. Some of them rambled
on at length, telling him things they had told him
on the previous round, but he never said so. Christina rather liked him; his temper didn't worry her
very much and since he had discovered that she

wasn't in the least afraid of him, he seldom vented
it upon her, and if he sometimes flew into a rage
with one of her nurses, then she stood up for her
with a cool determination which he had found difficult to dispose of. On the whole, the two of them
got on very well. He was on the point of leaving
the ward when he turned suddenly and addressed
her. 'I suppose it was you who diagnosed Mr Tate
for us, Sister?'

Her grey eyes were very clear. 'Dr Fisher was
concerned about him,' she told him quietly. 'He
told me when he came to examine him early this
morning that he had suspected a cerebral tumour,
sir.'

Dr Robinson nodded, swivelling his eyes behind
their glasses to look at Dr Fisher, as red as a tur-
key-cock.

'That's what I thought you'd say. Well, he's got
a chance now he's transferred to the surgical side.
Thanks to you,' he added sotto voce.

The day was uneventful after that. Christina
went down to her dinner presently, sharing a table
with several of her friends, talking shop interlarded
with clothes, boy-friends and holidays. Everyone
seemed to be going abroad. She looked round her
quite nonplussed when someone asked her where
she was going for her winter leave.

She said slowly: 'Well, I don't know—I hadn't
given it a thought. I expect George Henry will

want to stay at home, and I might go down to Somerset. It's nice at this time of year, though I've no holidays until the beginning of October.'

She thought about it once or twice during the afternoon. It would be fun to go away, abroad, perhaps, even Scotland or Wales. Perhaps she could persuade George Henry to come with her, she was sure he hadn't made any plans.

She couldn't have been more mistaken. They had had their supper and for once he had followed her into their small sitting room instead of going to his study and it seemed an opportunity to bring the matter up, but before she could start he said with unusual brusqueness: 'Chrissy, I want to talk to you... I've been meaning to tell you for a week or two, but somehow...I'm going to get married.'

He paused to look at her and was reassured to see that she was looking at him with a serene face. The light was dim, so he couldn't see how pale she had gone.

'You know her—Hilary Woods. We've had an understanding for some time now and last week we decided to marry as soon as possible. There's no point in waiting—she'll give up her job, of course, and live here.'

Christina had the extraordinary feeling that she was having a dream. The room didn't seem quite real, nor did George Henry, talking away so earnestly about getting married—and to Hilary

Woods, a social worker with a puffed-up sense of her own importance. She knew, without her brother saying a word, that she would have to leave before Hilary put a foot over the doorstep. She said in her calm way: 'George Henry, how super for you! I'm so glad—Hilary will make you a splendid wife and she'll be so understanding.'

George Henry eyed her carefully. 'Then you don't mind? I've been worried—you know, wondering if you'd mind—I mean, finding somewhere else to live. Hilary said you'd be able to get a room at St Athud's without any trouble at all. I daresay you'd like it better—you'd be independent and have a great deal more time for your own amusement.'

Briefly, she wondered what she would do with all the extra time. Perhaps it would be better if she could find a bedsitter or a tiny flat, but there would be lonely meals to eat and no one to talk to. She wasn't going to feel sorry for herself but facts would have to be faced.

'Well, of course I can—the Sisters' rooms are pretty good, you know, and I can take up tennis again and I've always wanted to join the Social Club.' She uttered the thumping lie without blinking and saw George Henry relax. 'When are you thinking of getting married?' she asked.

'Well, actually, in a month's time. We've already been about the licence. It's to be a quiet affair—just a few friends and Hilary's parents. You'll come, of course, Chrissy.'

'I wouldn't miss it for the world! I'll go and see someone about getting a room. Hilary will want to make some changes here, I expect, and it'll be much easier if I'm not here.'

'We don't want to turn you out.'

'You're not, my dear, and I'm delighted for you both—when you see Hilary tell her that, won't you? I wouldn't like her to be worried on my account.' Christina got up and went to look out of the window into the dull street beyond, suddenly filled with the crazy desire to leave it all; go somewhere far away, start again in another job, perhaps meet someone who would want to marry her— someone like Adam ter Brandt.

She went the next day to ask about living in. There was a room free, she was told, and she went to look at it. It was nicely furnished in an impersonal way with a view over the streets around the hospital, but the idea of living there, probably for years, appalled her. It was sheer good luck that at dinner time Linda Soames, one of the Accident Room Sisters, announced that she was leaving in a month's time and did anyone want to take over her bedsitter. 'It's five minutes' quick walk from here,' she observed, 'and on the top floor. The street's fairly quiet and there's a kind of kitchen in a cupboard and you share the bathroom.'

When Christina said that she was interested, the entire table turned to stare at her.

'But you live with your brother,' exclaimed Beryl. 'Has he sold the practice, then?'

'No, he's getting married.'

'But, Chrissy...' someone started, and then stopped as she went on:

'I'm so glad, I was beginning to think that he was a confirmed bachelor.'

There was a little silence until someone else said: 'Who's the lucky girl?'

'Hilary Woods—she's a social worker.' She added: 'Ideal for a doctor's wife.'

She told herself that several times during the next day or two. Hilary came to dinner and Christina didn't allow herself to be annoyed at any of the remarks that young lady made. It was obvious that George Henry was very much in love and if he was happy that was more important than anything else. She listened with composure while Hilary made suggestions about her future, giving advice where none was sought, and to give her her due, unaware that she was being unspeakably bossy. Christina replied suitably to all the sensible suggestions put to her and offered no information, nor did she show her annoyance when Hilary criticised the way in which the beef had been cooked, the arrangement of the furniture in the sitting-room and the cheerful clutter of ornaments scattered round it. The latter Christina intended to remove when she left; most of them were hers, anyway, treasures from a happy childhood and bits and pieces which had belonged to her mother. As to the tables and chairs, Hilary was welcome to do what she liked with them, and that went for the beef too. She endured another half an hour of patronage while they washed up and then went thankfully to her room, on the plea that she had a long day before her.

Carole had gone off sick the evening before and the only way to get round that was to do an eight-till-eight herself; there was no one available to take over from her if she went off duty, and she didn't really mind. All the same, she was tired when she got home just before nine o'clock to find a note from George Henry saying that he had taken Hilary out to dinner. Christina went into the kitchen and looked in the fridge. She couldn't face the beef, not after Hilary's expert criticism. An egg, she supposed, and some toast. The front door bell rang as she was getting out the bread and she went to answer it—if it was a patient they would have to telephone Dr Howes who shared emergency calls with George Henry, after eight o'clock.

Adam ter Brandt was on the doorstep. In one smooth movement he had kissed her surprised face, come inside and shut the door behind him.

'Hullo,' he said with a devastating charm which

left her speechless. 'Is George Henry in?' And when she shook her head, 'Good—pleased to see me? Where is he? On a case?'

She found her voice and she hoped it sounded as cool and matter-of-fact as usual. 'He's gone out to dinner with his fiancée.'

He pulled a face which made him look more devastating than ever.

'Going to marry? What about you?' He grinned at her. 'You'll never stay here as an uneasy third, will you?'

'Certainly not. I shall go into the Nurses' Home at the hospital or find a bedsitter.'

His blue eyes smiled into hers. 'But you don't want to, do you? Tell you what—let's go and have dinner somewhere and you shall tell me all about it?'

'I was just going to…' she began feebly, aware that she was ready to fly out of the door at that very moment.

'Never mind that. Get a jacket and powder your nose—we'll go now.'

He drove a rather showy Mercedes Benz 450SL, and he drove fast, but Christina didn't mind. She was blissfully happy; Adam had turned up again, quite miraculously, and for the moment the future didn't matter a row of pins.

But in the little Greek restaurant, over kebab and a bottle of wine, she found herself telling him everything, something which astonished her, for she hadn't confided in anyone, not even her closest friends, for years. She ended abruptly saying in a shamed voice: 'I'm sorry, Adam, I've been boring on, why on earth didn't you stop me?'

'I didn't want to. Besides, I've just had a perfectly splendid idea. How about coming to Holland and working for six months or a year?'

'Me? But I can't speak a word of Dutch!'

'That won't matter—you will be given a crash course. Do you speak any languages at all?'

'Not fluently. I did French and German for A levels…'

He switched to French. 'Do you have a liking for languages? Are you a quick student?'

She answered him in rather hesitant but correct French. 'Yes, I think so, but how would I manage while I was learning?'

'Everyone speaks English, especially in the hospitals, and almost all the medical terms are the same, only pronounced differently. You would get help.'

'I think I might like it very much.'

He was speaking German now. 'And I think you would do very well, Chrissy. Will you do it? I would like you to come very much.' His blue eyes sparkled and she smiled back at him.

'I'll think about it,' she told him in German.

'And not too long.' They were speaking English

now. 'It will be necessary for my partner—he's my brother, and the senior and Directeur of the hospital—to agree.'

'Oh, is he likely to object?'

Adam laughed. 'Not at all likely. He objects almost never—he is a calm man, so calm that sometimes one does not know what he is really thinking about, but I have no doubt that he will be glad to have you on the hospital staff. I shall be going to den Haag this weekend, I'll talk to him about it and let you know when I get back.'

She felt breathless. 'Yes, well—it does sound rather super.'

'Then that's settled. I shall be back in Holland in a few weeks now, but we'll see plenty of each other then, darling.'

Christina's cheeks pinkened, but she said with composure: 'Will you tell me something about Holland?' And while he talked she watched him, unable to take her eyes from his face. She was behaving like a teenage idiot, she admonished herself as they drove back, and she was enjoying it. And when Adam kissed her goodnight at her brother's door, she enjoyed that too.

CHAPTER TWO

THERE WERE three days until the weekend and Adam had said that he would return on the Monday, but Christina didn't allow herself to get excited. She went steadily about her work, and if in the solitude of her room she spent rather longer than usual doing things to her face and trying out different hair-styles that was her business and no one else's.

She remained calm, outwardly at least, when Monday came and went and there was no sign of Adam. She reminded herself of all the very good reasons why he hadn't come and went home on the Tuesday evening, telling herself that he would be there when she arrived, or telephone or even write…

He had done none of these things. Moreover, Hilary was there, making it plain that Christina was making a quite unnecessary third, hinting plainly that there was a splendid film on at the Odeon and wouldn't she like to see it.

'Funny you should have said that,' said Christina in a bright voice. 'I'm meeting some of the others in an hour, we're going to eat first, there's just time before the second house.'

So she went to her room and changed, wished them a pleasant evening and left the house. The last thing she wanted to do; she was tired and depressed and hungry, and worst of all, supposing Adam came while she was out? She took a bus to Tottenham Court Road and sat through a film she wasn't in the least interested in, eating a packet of sandwiches in the dark, because she hated going into cafés by herself.

She could hear voices from the sitting room as she let herself in later, so she shut the door loudly enough for them to hear her and then went in. George Henry and Hilary were sitting side by side looking at patterns of curtain material; obviously there had been no visitors. Christina said she'd had a lovely evening, wished them goodnight and whisked herself out of the room to make herself a pot of tea and carry it up to her room, together with the remains of a macaroni cheese from the fridge. It was quite late by now and it seemed rather a waste to fuss over her face and hair, because Adam wasn't coming. Probably the senior partner had overruled him, probably too he himself had thought better of it. Life, she reflected, was full of small disappointments, but it didn't do to grieve over them. She got into bed and went to sleep almost at once.

She wasn't on until ten o'clock the next morning, which gave her time to rush out and do some household shopping before she went on duty. She had two days off, starting on the next day, and she occupied herself in deciding what to do. Usually she had spent a good part of them at home, keeping George Henry company at meals and quite often going out in the evening if he was free, but now he had Hilary... A day's shopping, she thought; something new would be good for her and she could lunch at one of the big stores. She hadn't been to Harrods for a long time; she could spend the afternoon there and have tea, and since Beryl's steady had gone to Scotland for a week, she might spend the evening with her. There was another day to plan, of course, but that would do for the present.

The day seemed endless. The ward was full and several patients were very ill, so it was long after eight o'clock when she got off duty. She had to wait for a bus too and it had begun to rain a little as she walked the last stage of her journey. As she put her key in the door she thanked heaven that Hilary had gone to see her parents in Highgate. George Henry would have had his supper long since; she would boil herself an egg and would spend half an hour with him. She closed the door behind her and crossed the hall to the study; the vague murmur of voices would be the television— George Henry had the habit of switching it on and then walking away and forgetting all about it. She opened the door and went in.

Adam was there; she didn't see anyone or anything else for a few moments. Her face lighted up with her delight and she cried 'Adam, I thought you weren't coming…' before she realised that besides him and George Henry there was someone else in the room.

He had risen to his feet as she paused at the door, a tall man, taller than Adam and, unlike him, heavily built. He had the same handsome face, but his mouth was firm and his nose high-bridged; moreover, although his eyes were blue, they were pale and very clear. Christina wasn't sure about his hair; it was so fair that it could have been grey or just flaxen. He wasn't all that young either, in his thirties, and dressed with a conservative good taste very much in contrast to Adam's rather flamboyant clothes. She had the instant impression of quietness before George Henry spoke.

'Chrissy, how late you are. Adam has brought his brother to visit us to see you, actually.' He frowned a little. 'You didn't tell me you were considering taking a post in Holland.'

She smiled at him. 'Well, love, it seemed a bit silly to say anything before I knew more about it.'

She shook hands with Adam and turned to the other man. 'This is Duert—I told him about you, and he decided he might as well come back with me and see you.' Adam was still holding her hand and she pulled it away gently, to be engulfed in a very large firm one.

'So much more satisfactory than writing letters and filling in forms.' His voice was deep and pleasant and he had a nice smile. He was looking at her in what she considered to be a vague fashion. 'I'm sorry we didn't give you a reasonable warning that we were coming perhaps we might meet and discuss this matter of a job?'

His straight eyebrows rose in faint query and she answered seriously: 'Of course. I have a free day tomorrow.'

'We can have lunch,' interposed Adam. 'I'll be free for a couple of hours.'

'Then perhaps you could spare me an hour in the afternoon?'

Christina gave him a long calm look. 'You mean there's a chance of me getting a job at the hospital?'

'There is a strong possibility, but we do need to talk about it.' He gave her a lazy smile, friendly enough but not very interested. And she could hardly blame him; she must look pretty awful with damp hair and her face still wet from the rain. She said formally, 'That would suit me very well, Dr ter Brandt, if you would tell me where I am to meet you.'

'Oh, I'll pick you up directly after you've lunched with Adam.'

George Henry had been sitting back listening. Now he said: 'You're sure you want this, Chrissy? It's not just because Hilary and I are getting married? You said that you had the chance of a bedsitter or a room at St Athud's…'

'Oh, yes, I know,' she answered him with her usual calm air, 'but you see I wasn't sure, it was only a suggestion on Adam's part, but I really want to go, George Henry. A change will do me good—I'm getting in a rut.'

The three men looked at her, her brother with surprise because she had never before even hinted that she was dissatisfied with her job, Adam with lighthearted amusement, and Duert ter Brandt with a bland face and thoughtful eyes.

It was he who broke the silence with a casual: 'Well, we'll talk about it tomorrow, shall we?'

He held out a hand. 'I hope we haven't trespassed for too long upon your leisure. Goodnight, Miss Forbes.' He shook hands with George Henry too and Christina barely had the time to say goodbye to Adam before they went. Duert ter Brandt could at least have given them the chance to talk for a few minutes, instead of which he swept Adam out of the house with an authority, which although not apparent was nonetheless very real.

After they had gone she remembered that Adam

hadn't told her where and when they were to meet for lunch. She was still digesting this when George Henry observed: 'I like him—Adam's brother, a nice unassuming chap.'

She answered him tartly: 'A bit too suave for me, but I'm not likely to see much of him if I get the job. He's the hospital director and presumably he does his directing from some office or other.'

George Henry fiddled with a pen lying on his desk. 'Have you any details of the job? The ward you'll be on, off duty, salary and so on?'

'None at all. Adam told me that there were vacancies at the hospital and that I might suit, but it was for Dr ter Brandt to decide. He wanted to know if I could speak French or German and he seemed quite satisfied with my efforts. It was really to see if I had any aptitude for languages, I think it seems you're given a crash course in Dutch.'

Her brother frowned. 'You really want to go, Chrissy?'

She turned an eager face to his. 'Oh, George Henry, yes!'

She was aware that her enthusiasm was largely due to the likelihood of seeing Adam again, and quite often too. She told herself sternly that she would have to be sensible about that, but that didn't prevent her, when she was getting ready for bed, from taking a long look at her face, close up to the dressing table looking-glass and with a bright light showing it up. Her eyes were all right, but the rest of her was mediocre; she had a creamy unblemished skin, but she didn't consider that that helped at all—and her teeth were good, but she couldn't be expected to smile all the time. Her nose was unimportant and her mouth was wide and her hair, inclined to curl if left to itself, had been pulled back severely for so long now that it had grown like it. She peered anxiously at herself and wondered what Adam saw in her, if indeed he saw anything at all. But he had squeezed her fingers when they had shaken hands and smiled at her in a way to make her wonder if he liked her a little. Perhaps she would know tomorrow.

'Well, what do you think of her?' asked Adam as he drove the BMW too fast away from the dull streets towards the West End.

His brother said slowly: 'She seems a sensible young woman.'

Adam laughed, 'And plain with it, but the most gorgeous eyes—but perhaps you didn't notice them. I bet she's never been chatted up in her life—and she's not so young either. Very rewarding material to work on.'

Dr ter Brandt said evenly: 'Do not make the mistake of thinking that she is like the rest of your girl-friends, Adam. She is unsophisticated, I grant you; she is also calm and matter-of-fact. Moreover, I have it from her brother that she is a very capable

Ward Sister and thought highly of at the hospital. As you so ungallantly point out, she is neither very young nor pretty, and definitely not your cup of tea.' He added, still without heat: 'I think you should leave her alone.'

'Oh, don't worry, Duert, I haven't got designs on the girl, but she doesn't seem to have had much fun. A few dinners and an occasional evening out will do her the world of good. You'll consider her for a job?'

'Yes, I think I may. It rather depends on what experience she's had in the Accident Room and surgery.' The big man heaved his bulk out of the car as Adam stopped in front of Brown's Hotel and then turned to ask: 'Where are you taking her to lunch?'

'Oh, a little Greek place in Soho—' Adam gave its name and at the look of surprise on his brother's face added testily: 'Well, she's not used to the Ritz or Claridge's, she might feel awkward.' He looked away from the pale blue eyes staring at him so steadily. 'What time will you meet us?'

'I will be there at half past two. I think I may go back in the evening so see that you're punctual. What time do your afternoon lectures start?'

'A quarter to three.' Adam sounded sulky.

'In that case you had better be outside this place by two-fifteen.'

Dr ter Brandt turned on his heel and went into the hotel without looking back.

Adam telephoned quite early the following morning so that Christina had plenty of time in which to decide what she should wear. None of her clothes were very exciting, although they were good and in excellent taste. It was cool and cloudy so that she felt justified in wearing the suit she had bought only a few weeks earlier. It was grey flannel with a pleated skirt and a neat little jacket and she had a silk blouse in a pale silvery grey to go with it. She dressed with care, made sure that George Henry's lunch was ready for him, and left the house. Adam had said he couldn't fetch her, so she took a bus to Oxford Street and then walked the rest of the way through the crowded Soho streets.

The restaurant was small and faintly shabby as to paint, but it had tubs of flowers each side of the door and the net curtains at the windows were a pristine white. She was aware of a vague disappointment and the thought shot through her head that she need not have put on her new suit; she felt overdressed, what with the silk blouse and the patent leather shoes and handbag, when as far as she could see every other girl in sight was wearing jeans or some long flowing garment with a lot of bracelets.

But she forgot all that as Adam crossed the

pavement to meet her and took her arm. 'What a punctual girl!' he greeted her. 'I was afraid you might be late, girls so often are—and I have to be gone again by a quarter past two.' He saw the look of doubt on her face and added: 'Oh, it's all right, Duert will be here to collect you and put you through your paces.'

They had gone inside and been given a little table at the back of the little restaurant, and when Christina put her hands on the table, Adam had covered them with his own so that all the questions she was going to ask him flew out of her head. All the same, she didn't allow herself to get carried away, although her heart was thundering in her ears. After a moment she gently withdrew her hands and looked around her. The place was a lot nicer inside than it was outside, she decided, and the waiter who served them was quick and attentive. She chose a fish salad and a fresh fruit salad and drank the wine she was offered without knowing what it was.

Adam didn't talk about the possibility of her getting a job, only discussed in a charming if vague fashion the various places he intended to take her to once she was in Holland. She was too sensible to believe quite all he said, although she would have liked to, but even if they only did half the things he was enthusing about, the future seemed to her to be an enchantment not to be missed. The time slid away too quickly and it was Adam who looked at his watch and said: 'Oh, lord—it's time we went.'

She put down her coffee cup in an unflurried manner. 'Very well. I'm going to powder my nose.'

'Must you?' He sounded irritable, but at her look of surprise he said: 'Sorry—I didn't mean to snap, but don't be too long, will you?'

The wine had flushed her cheeks a little, but otherwise she looked as well groomed as when she had left home that morning. She poked at her hair, put on more lipstick and rejoined Adam.

Dr Duert ter Brandt was standing on the edge of the pavement outside, his back to the restaurant. It was a very large back and very straight in its beautifully tailored jacket. He must have had eyes at the back of his head, for he turned round before they reached him, wished her a friendly good afternoon, said something in a soft voice to Adam and lifted his hand at a passing taxi. Once more barely given time to say more than goodbye to Adam, Christina found herself sitting back beside Dr ter Brandt.

'I thought that we might walk in Green Park,' his voice was quiet and slow after Adam's quick, accented English. 'You understand that there are a number of questions I must ask you? And if we are both satisfied I shall require references.'

She said yes a little breathlessly; funny to think that only a few days ago she had been contemplating a dull future in a bedsitter. But she hadn't got the job yet.

It was pleasant in the park; they strolled through its comparative peace while the doctor asked questions. A great many questions, thought Christina, answering them in her sensible manner, giving him facts and taking care not to boast or pretend about anything.

'And surgery?' he wanted to know.

'Not for the last two years, I'm afraid. I had the Women's Surgical Ward for two years before I got my present post, and before that I was in Casualty and the Accident Room, a year as Second Sister and previous to that about a year as a staff nurse.'

'You like accident work?'

'Yes, very much. I should have liked to have stayed on there, but I was advised that I should get all-round experience. I haven't been at St Athud's all the time, you know. I came to London when my parents died and took the job I have got now. Before then I was living near Yeovil. I worked at the hospital there, but I trained at Bart's.'

They had stopped to watch an old man feeding the birds and presently Dr ter Brandt said: 'The post I have to offer you is that of Third Sister in the Accident Department at the Theofilus Hospital. We operate three shifts in the twenty-four hours, and you would be expected to work each shift in turn. You would have two days off each week, six weeks' holiday in the year and for the first few months at least, attend classes in Dutch. You may live in the hospital if you wish or rent rooms or a flat close by.' He mentioned a salary which, changed into English money, seemed generous.

'But perhaps the cost of living is higher?' asked Christina, sensibly.

'About the same, I think.'

She said composedly: 'I may apply for the post?'

'Yes. I have an application form with me, which we will fill in presently. The post is vacant now, but of course you will have to resign—a month, I take it?'

The old man had gone and so had the birds. A cool wind rustled the trees around them and a few leaves fluttered on to the grass. Christina said in her sensible way: 'I have more than two weeks' holiday due to me, which means that I can leave in about ten days' time.'

'That would suit us very well.' He paused and added thoughtfully: 'But of course you would like to stay here until your brother's marriage?'

'No.' Her voice was level and quiet. 'That doesn't matter. I should explain that my brother and I are very fond of each other and we get on very well. I'm delighted that he's marrying, but his fiancée and I—well, we don't get on very well. I think it might be easier for all of us if I'm not at the wedding.' She added slowly, 'We haven't quarrelled or anything like that, but George Henry feels a bit mean because I'm having to find somewhere else to live and it would be a good thing if I'm not there to remind him…'

The doctor's smile was kind. 'I'm sorry, but thank you for telling me; I'm sure it's a sensible solution. These unfortunate occasions do arise, but I've found that time does much to improve them.'

'That's what I thought. By the time I get back to England it will be forgotten.' They had been strolling along, but now she stopped. 'I've taken up your afternoon, Dr ter Brandt. If there's nothing more I need to know, I'll say goodbye. I'm sure I can manage the form and I'll get the references and send them on to you.'

For answer he took her arm. 'A cup of tea, I think, and we can fill in the form at the same time.'

He walked her back across the park and into Piccadilly, crossed the street and ushered her through the splendid entrance of the Ritz. 'Tea here?' she asked uncertainly.

'It's the nicest place I know of for tea,' he told her as they were led to a table by the window.

Christina had gone past the hotel many times since she had been in London, but never been inside. It was splendid and elegant and everything she had imagined it would be, and she was glad that she was wearing the grey suit; there wasn't a pair of denims in sight, the atmosphere was peaceful and restful, and having taken it all in she said forthrightly: 'This is delightful. I've often wondered what it was like inside, and now I know.'

And when the tea came she poured it with a dignified self-assurance which gave the lie to Adam's theory that she might feel ill at ease in such plushy surroundings. The doctor, plying her with wafer-thin cucumber sandwiches, little iced cakes and tiny meringues, looked at her with approval. She was no fool, this rather plain girl with the lovely eyes; she had a delightful voice and nice manners and a sensible head on her shoulders. And he liked the way she dressed too. She had a good figure and small, well kept hands. After a time, he mused, one forgot her lack of looks and probably, given enough incentive, she could improve on those.

He had an uneasy feeling that Adam was going to provide that incentive, and although, as he had said before, she seemed capable of looking after herself, she was too honest and nice a girl to be hurt. Of course, Adam might be serious about her; she was so very different from the usual kind of girl he fell in love with, it might be possible. Time would tell.

He asked casually: 'Are you meeting Adam this evening, Christina?'

She shook her head. 'No, he's got a lecture and he had to catch up on something he missed—and tomorrow he has a study day at Birmingham.'

The doctor sat back, his eyes on her face. 'I have to stay in London until tomorrow evening. Perhaps we might have lunch together, then if there are any snags or problems we can sort them out.'

'Thank you, I should like that.' Her gaze met his and she smiled. 'Should I fill in that form?'

They did it together, laughing a little while Christina tried to remember dates and how tall she was and the exact date upon which she had started her training. It was finished at last and she was surprised to find that they had been sitting over their tea for more than an hour. And she had enjoyed herself; her companion had turned out to be nicer than she had expected; rather reserved, perhaps, but he must be a good deal older than Adam. He would be comfortably married, of course; she had taken that for granted. She would have like to have asked him if he had any children, but she had already formed the impression that his private life was very much his own business.

They took a taxi back to George Henry's house after that, but the doctor, politely opening the door for her, refused her invitation to come in, pleading an evening engagement and wishing her a pleasantly impersonal goodbye as he went. Christina stood in the hall, listening to the coughs and murmurs coming from the waiting room, already stuffed with the evening surgery patients. She felt as though a door, briefly opened on to another world, had been gently but inexorably closed again.

'It's not my world anyway,' she reminded herself sensibly, and went upstairs to change the grey suit for a skirt and jumper and then went along to the kitchen to see about supper.

Hilary came that evening and displayed an unflattering amazement that anyone should want to take Christina to the Ritz for tea. She said, her rather prominent blue eyes narrowed: 'Well, really, whatever next? Was he trying to impress you?'

Christina considered the question. 'No—he's not that kind of man. I think it was because the Ritz was close by and it was tea time and I had to fill in a form. We had to have a table, you see.'

Hilary gave her a suspicious glance, but Christina appeared to be serious, so she gave a reluctant nod. 'Dead set on this job, aren't you? Supposing you hate it when you're there?'

Christina allowed herself a silent giggle. Hilary's face showed very plainly that she wished she hadn't said that; supposing Christina said that she would return home and expect to live with her and George Henry until she found another job to suit her? She said gently: 'Well, you know, Hilary, I'm a bit slow about making up my mind about places and people—other people know within seconds if they like something or someone, but not me.' She remembered very clearly that she had known within a second that she liked Adam, but of course there was always the exception to every rule...'I shall enjoy the experience,' she finished.

Hilary agreed with eager enthusiasm and hardly concealed her pleasure when Christina mentioned that it wasn't likely that she would be at the wedding. George Henry, Christina decided, must be very in love not to notice, but that was a good thing. She was a firm believer in love, herself unloved.

'You won't come back,' observed Hilary in a satisfied voice.

'Probably not, and certainly not to London.' Christina beamed at them both. 'Have you decided what you would like for a present?' she asked.

Dr ter Brandt came for her at noon the next day, keeping the taxi waiting outside while he chatted amiably with George Henry, who had just come in from an emergency call. Which gave Christina time to take another quick look at herself in the old-fashioned wardrobe mirror. She was wearing the suit again because it seemed suitable in the elegant company of the doctor, and she wondered where they were to lunch.

She hadn't included Claridge's in her guessing. She got out of the taxi and looked up at its solid imposing front, then she looked at the doctor.

'Will I do for a place like this?' she asked simply.

He looked her up and down very deliberately. 'Very well indeed,' he assured her, and she said matter-of-factly:

'Oh, that's all right, then. I shouldn't like to let you down.'

They had a table by the window again, shown to it by the manager of the restaurant, who greeted the doctor with the smiling respect due to a regular visitor. There was a band playing softly somewhere and the restaurant was elegant and quiet. Christina sighed as she sat down.

'This is very delightful,' she observed, 'and a bit exciting to me. I expect you come here a lot?'

'From time to time. What would you like to drink?' And when she hesitated: 'A dry sherry would give us an appetite, if you'd care for that?'

'Please.' She added with disarming frankness: 'I don't know much about drinks.'

'Then you'll allow me to guide you.' He took the menu he had been offered and glanced across at her, already studying hers.

'I'm famished,' he told her placidly. 'I shall have a steak, but how about a starter? Avocado, perhaps?' and when she agreed, relieved to have some guidance through the enormous selection of food, 'If you like fish, I can recommend the salmon, or perhaps lobster?'

'Salmon, please.' She wasn't absolutely sure what you did with a lobster. She sat back and looked around her and the doctor looked at her. She had self-possession, that was evident, and no pretence. He had expected her to tell him that she didn't know what to do with a lobster and he was quite disappointed because she hadn't. She wasn't gauche, he decided, merely deprived of the usual opportunities most girls had of going out and picking up these useful pieces of information. He would warn Adam not to make the mistake of taking her to a second class restaurant again. She would be able to cope with Buckingham Palace if necessary because she had sense and natural good manners and an honesty which he found rather touching. He couldn't think of any of his women friends, offhand, who would have stopped outside a restaurant in order to ask if they would do.

He elaborated upon the job she had applied for while they ate their way through the most delicious lunch she had ever tasted, and watching the light-as-air profiteroles being piled on to her plate, she remarked: 'It all sounds quite splendid—but the thing is, I'm so taken up with this gorgeous food I don't think I'm appreciating it as I should.'

The doctor gave a great booming laugh. 'Then

I shall have to send you a job description leaflet when I get back.'

Which reminded her to ask: 'You're going this evening?'

'Yes, I must.' He didn't tell her that he had stayed another day so that he might take her out to lunch. He had been sorry for her, but he wasn't any more. She was one of those calm, sensible girls who didn't allow themselves to become flustered. Adam would try and charm her out of that calmness, but Duert doubted if he would succeed. He would make sure that he didn't anyway; she was too nice a girl to have her heart broken by the carefree Adam. There were plenty of girls who could play his game and not get hurt. The doctor, whose own tastes ran to sophisticated women whose witty conversation kept him mildly amused and who were never surprised or excited about anything at all, glanced at Christina with puzzled eyes. There was absolutely nothing about this dab of a girl to interest him, so why had he taken her out to lunch? To save her from the disappointment of not seeing Adam, he supposed idly.

'Adam will be back tomorrow,' he told her, and watched her face light up. 'He has only three more weeks here; you will be quite at home in den Haag by then.'

She poured their coffee with a steady hand while she contemplated her exciting future. 'So I shall,'

she told him. 'When will I know? I have to resign…'

'Oh, do that tomorrow, will you?' and at her
look of surprise, 'I've recommended you for the
post and I'm the director of the hospital, so the
job's yours, Christina. Let me know when you can
come and I'll arrange to have you met. You'll need
a passport, of course; I'll see about your work per-
mit. Have you enough money for your fare or
would you like an advance?'

'I've enough, thank you.'

'Good—well, we'll see how you get on, shall
we? If at the end of a month you're not happy, let
me know.'

'And if I don't suit?' she prompted.

'Then I shall let you know.'

She wouldn't like that to happen. He seemed
such an easygoing man, but she suspected that
upon occasion he could be icy-tempered, venting
his rage in a cold voice on whoever had been hap-
less enough to incur his displeasure. Christina
hoped most sincerely that she would never be un-
lucky enough to do that, and anyway, she wouldn't
see much of him once she was there. She didn't
know much about hospital directors, but she hardly
thought he would do anything else but administra-
tive work.

There didn't seem much more to say after that.
She finished her coffee, invented a meeting with

one of the Sisters from the hospital, wished him a pleasant journey back home, thanked him for her delightful lunch and assured him that she really had to go. She wasn't surprised when he at once asked for the bill, paid it and ushered her out of the restaurant; indeed, she was a little worried as to whether she had lingered too long, which made her goodbyes rather brisk.

'I'll get you a taxi,' offered the doctor, and when she said no, thank you, she would walk as it was close by, and he asked where, his eyes gleamed with amusement when she said wildly: 'Oh, Piccadilly Circus,' which wasn't close by at all.

He stood on the pavement and watched her walk briskly to the corner and into Davies Street, on her way to the crowds and bustle of Oxford Street. He very much doubted if she was going to meet anyone.

Christina got on a bus when she reached Oxford Street and went home; it was mid-afternoon, George Henry was out on his afternoon visits and she had the house to herself. She sat down at the dining room table and made a list of all the things she had to do within the next few days, then she wrote a letter of resignation ready to hand in in the morning, made a cup of tea, washed her hair and then sat down again and allowed herself to indulge in daydreams just a little. Adam cropped up in all of them.

CHAPTER THREE

HALFWAY THROUGH the next ten days Christina took stock of her situation, not because she was having second thoughts or suffering from nerves but so that she might check on her preparations. She had had confirmation of her appointment at the Theofilus Hospital, together with a letter of businesslike brevity, telling her how, when and where to travel. She had also had rather a nasty interview with the Principal Nursing Officer, who took it as a personal affront that Christina should want to leave St Athud's, and she had borne with equanimity the endless questions and comments from her various friends and acquaintances, not to mention the rather anxious ones from Hilary, obviously terrified that she might change her mind at the last moment.

She had done some shopping too; a couple of dresses, one a soft green jersey the other a two-piece in silvery grey. These, reinforced by a handful of woollies and blouses from Marks and Spencers, last year's tweed skirt and some slacks would do very well for a start, she considered, and then after due consideration, went out and bought a long dark green velvet skirt and a very expensive silk blouse with lace insertions to go with it. She packed the lot together with undies, raincoat and a variety of footwear and declared herself ready.

Of Adam she had seen very little, but perhaps that was a good thing, for she had had quite a lot to do and the ward was full again. When he did telephone and suggest dinner she had had to refuse because her friends were giving her a farewell party, a rather noisy female affair which she had very much enjoyed. But on the following evening she was free and they had dined at a small French restaurant. On an impulse Christina had taken the new green jersey from her case and worn it, and had taken extra pains with her face and hair. Used to her brother's laconic praise of anything new, she wasn't too disappointed at Adam's casual: 'You look nice.'

She listened happily to his lighthearted account of his studies, what he intended to do when they were finished, and his plans for a holiday on Tenerife, and she was quite breathless with happiness when he suggested carelessly that she might like to go too.

'There'll be half a dozen of us,' he told her. 'We'll fly over, of course.' Luckily he didn't wait for her reply but rattled on about something else, which gave her time to reflect sadly that she hadn't a hope of going with him. But she didn't stay sad for long; after all, she would be seeing quite a lot of him when she got to Holland. The thought brought colour to her cheeks and made her eyes sparkle so that Adam paused in what he was saying to remark. 'You know, Chrissy, if you'd do something to your hair you'd be quite pretty.'

It was astonishing to her what an effect he had upon her usual calm. Her pink cheeks got a good deal pinker, although she tried to keep her voice light. 'I had it permed once, and I looked frightful, besides—I was quite hopeless at setting it.'

Adam looked surprised. 'Don't you want to make the most of yourself?' His smile was charming. 'For me, Chrissy? Buy some pretty clothes and have your hair done and use more make-up,' he coaxed her.

She said soberly: 'But then it wouldn't be me.'

He studied her with narrowed eyes. 'How old are you?' and when she told him: 'Three years older than I, but you've the naïveté of a girl of seventeen. I shall have to take you in hand.'

He said it lightly and laughed as he spoke, but he stretched out a hand and caught hers across the table, stroking it gently with a finger. Christina drew her hand away. 'It wouldn't be any good,' she told him matter-of-factly, 'I'm too old to change my ways.'

'If that's a challenge, I'll accept it,' he said at once. 'When you get to Holland, I'll take you to a really super hairdresser in the Hague; he'll do wonders for you, and a girl I know goes to a beauty parlour there. She'll take you along with her on a visit to a boutique and you won't know yourself, darling.'

It sounded too good to be true, and lying in bed later, she decided that it was. Even if she'd possessed the kind of money she would obviously have to spend to change herself into the kind of girl Adam admired, she was fairly certain that no amount of beauty treatment would turn her into someone glamorous everyone—and everyone was Adam, of course—would fall for at the first glance. All the same, she decided just before she fell asleep, she would go and have her hair decently cut and set and lay out what money she could spare on more make-up.

She went two days later—to a wildly expensive hairdresser her friends assured her was absolutely terrific. Not that the great man actually did more than spend a few minutes staring at her and then muttering instructions to the assistant. Probably he felt disheartened at what he saw, thought Christina, afterwards, for although her hair was trimmed it was still long and it had merely been washed and set so that the faint natural wave in it was given a chance to show itself, but at least the assistant had dressed it in a much softer style. Everyone agreed, when she displayed herself at supper that evening, that the astronomical sum she had paid had been worth it just for the new style alone. Christina, peering at herself in the glass, hoped so too.

She was to meet Adam once more before she left for Holland. He had no time, he explained on the telephone, but perhaps they could meet for drinks, just for an hour. She was free that afternoon, and encouraged by the visit to the hairdresser's, she rushed off to a beauty parlour, where a supercilious young woman examined her face from all angles, pointed out its defects with the remark: 'I always think it's best to tell the truth, don't you, madam?' and then went to work with a will. Christina was almost afraid to look in the mirror when she was finished, and when she did she gave a gasp. The face looking back at her was hers, all right, but now she had long dark eyelashes, a mouth which wasn't at all the same shape as it had been and a green eye-shadow which she wasn't sure that she liked. Indeed, she felt quite uneasy, and in half a mind to take the whole lot off, but the young woman, standing back to admire her handiwork, assured her that the improvement was quite fantastic, which wasn't really very flattering, and then sold her a lipstick and the eye-shadow she didn't like. Christina went on duty feeling extremely self-conscious and then was considerably heartened by a visit from Beryl, come to borrow some catheters, who declared that she looked quite super and on no account was she ever to go back to her old ways.

Christina laughed, 'Well, I'll not get much time to do all this every day,' she pointed out, 'but I'll do my best if you think it's really made a difference.'

And it must have done, for when Willie Fisher came to see his patients just before she went off duty he stared at her quite openly and muttered: 'You look different.'

It was a pity that Adam, when they met later that evening, said nothing at all, even though Christina had made a point of choosing a seat under a bright light so that she was clearly visible. He was full of some disagreement he had had with someone or other who was at the same course as he: he didn't make it clear who the someone was or why they had disagreed, only that he had been right and they had been wrong. She listened with sympathy, forgetting her disappointment, so that it was all the more acute when he said presently: 'Well, you're off in a couple of days, aren't you, darling? I'll be seeing you in Holland, and remember what I said about taking you to a good hairdresser and getting some decent clothes.' They were on the pavement waiting for a taxi to take her back to St Athud's, and before she could answer that, one had drawn up and Adam had opened its door, kissed her and popped her inside. 'Can't wait to see you again,' he said in a voice which sounded convincingly sincere. She treasured the words as the taxi bore her away.

The next day was the last one before she left London. She and George Henry and Hilary had dinner together, making the kind of animated conversation usual to such an occasion. Hilary, with the wedding only a week or so away, was disposed to be friendly, and annoyingly patronising too. Christina bore with it meekly because she didn't want to hurt George Henry's feelings. He was still feeling guilty, although she had been careful never to give him reason to do so. So the three of them laughed and talked and made little jokes about Christina having to learn Dutch, and Hilary observed with more than a touch of spite that probably she would meet some Dutchman or other and marry him and never come back to England.

She said it with a laugh, but Christina thought it was the one thing that Hilary would like to happen, at the same time making it plain that the chance of it happening was a remote one.

She left for Heathrow Airport the next morning, outwardly composed but inwardly wildly excited. Watching England disappear from under her, she had no qualms about leaving London. She would miss her brother and her friends, but if she had regrets it was for her home in Somerset. But even if she had stayed in London, her chances of returning there were small. Perhaps she would be able to return there for a holiday some time.

The flight was brief; she found herself in the reception hall at Schiphol, standing by the reception desk as she had been told to do, awaiting whoever it was who was to meet her.

She hadn't long to wait. A short stout man with a round cheerful face, dressed with great neatness in a navy blue suit, touched her on the arm.

'Miss Forbes? I am sent by Dr ter Brandt to meet you and take you to the hospital. My name is Corvinus—I am his butler.'

His English was good, although the accent was strong and a little difficult to understand, but Christina was so relieved to hear her mother tongue that she barely noticed that. She said, 'How do you do,' politely, and added: 'What do I call you? Instead of mister, I mean.'

He looked faintly shocked. 'Corvinus, miss.' He picked up her case and took her overnight bag from her hand. 'If you will follow me…'

He led her through the crowds and outside to where a Daimler Sovereign was parked. And very nice too, thought Christina. Dr ter Brandt must be doing very well for himself. The stout man opened the door with a flourish, but she said at once, 'Oh, no—if you don't mind I'd rather sit with you.' The idea of being driven, sitting in state on the back seat, to her new job didn't seem right at all.

He beamed at her, 'A pleasure, miss,' installed her into the front seat and got in beside her.

'Is it far?' asked Christina.

'No, miss, but the traffic is very great.' He drove smoothly away. 'Fifty-six kilometres only, and that on the motorway.'

Where the speed limit didn't matter overmuch, she decided a few minutes later; the traffic was going at a furious pace and her companion with it. She glanced around her. Motorways were the same the world over, she mused, cutting through the country, rushing past half-hidden villages and towns. She studied several distant church spires and wondered about them. As though he had read her thoughts Corvinus said: 'Den Haag is a beautiful city and the country round it is beautiful also.'

'Oh, good.' She turned to smile at him. 'Your English is very good. Have you lived in England?'

'Yes, for a time, and also for holidays. My wife is English.'

Just hearing him say that made her feel much more at home. She didn't suppose she would ever meet that lady, but nonetheless it gave her a comforting glow. 'Oh, that is nice,' she declared warmly.

Corvinus drove fast; they were approaching the outskirts of den Haag in no time at all. Christina looked around her with interest; this was going to be her home for some time and she was determined to like it. There was no sign of the beautiful country she had been promised, but Corvinus assured her that on the other side of the city, along the coast, there were wide avenues of trees and a good deal of wooded land. 'And Scheveningen,' he pointed out, 'that is also delightful, and also Wassenaar. They are to be reached with ease from den Haag. And even in the city there are great open...' he paused for a word and she helped him out:

'Do you mean a kind of park? Like Hampstead Heath in London?'

'That is it. They are beautiful, the woods, and there are walks there.'

She looked backwards over her shoulder as he drove past the Haagsche Bos. The woods did indeed look lovely, the leaves already turning red and gold, soon lost to sight as Corvinus turned towards the city centre. After a few minutes he drove slowly down a narrow lane, turned into a wide, busy thoroughfare and so to a wide sweep before the hospital. It was a modern building, nine stories high and built in a slender curve. Christina stared up at it with interest. It presented a challenge to her and while feeling nervous at meeting a lot of new faces, she was determined to make a success of the job. She thanked Corvinus as she got out of the car, and he said: 'I wish you happiness, miss,' and carried her bags up the shallow steps and into the enormous reception hall, where he went straight to the porter's lodge, handed her over to the dignified personage who presided over it, and with a quiet goodbye, went away.

She watched him go with real regret. He had been friendly and reassuring and it would have been nice to have had him by her for a little longer. The head porter recalled her to her surroundings with faint impatience.

'Come with me, miss,' he advised her, and led the way across the hall to a line of lifts.

'Where am I going?' asked Christina.

'The Directrice.'

The one bit she had been rather dreading, but better to get it over with. They went two floors up and then walked down a long chilly passage lined with doors. The porter knocked on the last one and when the green light above it came on, opened it and stood aside for her to go in.

The room was spartan and its occupant rather matched her surroundings. She was a tall thin woman of indeterminate age, with large bony features, greying hair drawn back from a high forehead and beautiful bright blue eyes. She was dressed severely in a dark blue uniform with an old-fashioned starched cap on her head and bows under her determined chin. Christina took one look and liked her.

Her English was good but not fluent as she greeted Christina gravely, bade her be seated and then looked her over without haste. 'Dr ter Brandt recommends you highly,' she observed in a pleasant voice, 'and we are happy to have you with us. There will be a trial period of one month, at the end of which time either side may terminate the contract. After which we would wish you to give three months' notice if you should want to leave.'

'Yes, he did explain that to me,' said Christina, 'and I agreed to that.'

She waited composedly for the Directrice to speak.

'You will report for duty tomorrow morning at eight o'clock. The senior Hoofd Zuster, Zuster Kaarsen, will show you your duties and arrange your free time. You will find your uniform ready for you in your room. Please come and see me if you wish help at any time.' She glanced at the clock. 'The midday meal is finished, but something will be brought to your room and you will be free to unpack and do as you wish for the rest of this day.' She smiled and nodded dismissal. 'I hope that you will be very happy here, Miss Forbes.'

Outside the door once more, Christina found a small round little lady waiting for her. She shook hands and said in a cosy voice, 'Hoofd Zuster Zande—no English.'

'Christina Forbes—no Dutch,' said Christina gravely, and allowed herself to be led back down the corridor and into a lift once more. This time it was the top floor they went to, where the nurses had their rooms, and they went up and down a number of passages and lobbies before her guide finally stopped before an open door leading to a wide corridor. '*Hoofd Zusters*,' she explained, and unlocked a door. The room was quite large and comfortably furnished with a view of the city below which was quite breathtaking. It was a pity that Christina disliked heights; she took a brief glimpse out of the window and turned back to the room.

Zuster Zande flung open a door, revealing a small shower room, and then crossed to the built-in cupboard and opened it to show the uniforms hung tidily away. She smiled brightly, nodded her head, said '*Eten*,' and rustled away, leaving Christina to wonder what she had said. It was all very well to have a dictionary; she had learnt as many useful words as she had had the time for, now she suspected that the written word was a very different kettle of fish from the spoken one. She hoped that it meant food, and she was proved right, for a few minutes later there was a knock on the door and a young girl in a print dress and apron came in with a tray.

There were rolls filled with ham and cheese, a salad in a small bowl, and a large rosy apple, and better than all these, there was a pot of tea with sugar and milk. Christina, who had been warned by a friend who had holidayed in Holland that year that there was no milk served with the tea, heaved a sigh of relief, took off her jacket, and sat down at the little desk to eat her lunch. The tea was hot and strong and there was plenty of it; perhaps her friend had stayed in some remote place where tea wasn't easily obtainable. She drank the pot dry and turned to her unpacking and then to trying on her uniform. It fitted very well and she loved the starched caps with their brief muslin veils just covering the nape of her neck. The new hair-style suited them very well. She put everything ready for the morning and decided that she would go out.

She was getting into her jacket again when there was another knock on the door and two girls came in. They were about her own age, fair and pretty and blue-eyed and friendly. They introduced themselves as Leenie and Truus, and Leenie said as they shook hands, 'Our English is not good, but a little, you understand? We are now free and we wish to take you out.' She beamed at Christina, who beamed back,

'Oh, how very kind of you, I'd love that.'

'We go to change our clothes,' said Leenie. 'I am Hoofd Zuster of the Men's Surgical Ward, and Truus is Hoofd Zuster in the Accident Room—she works with you.' She added: 'Her English is not so good.'

Truus bearing this out, echoed, 'Not good,' and smiled.

'I must learn Dutch,' declared Christina, 'just as soon as I can. Is it difficult?'

'Not for us,' said Leenie, and went off into peals of laughter. 'You will have lessons.'

The three of them left the hospital presently, carrying on a lively conversation which involved a good deal of miming and hand-waving and laughter. Dr ter Brandt, pausing briefly at a first floor window as he took a teaching round in the Children's Unit, watched them go.

There were no other English nurses at the hospital, Christina learned at breakfast the next morning. She sat between Truus and Leenie at a round table for twelve and was introduced in turn to the other occupants, all of them *Hoofd Zusters* in wards or departments. They all spoke English too, although they assured her that once she started her lessons they would make a point of speaking Dutch to her. They were nice to her, friendly and helpful and full of hospital gossip, and she left the table with them, looking forward to her first day. The senior *Hoofd Zuster* in the Accident Room was a dragon, she had been told, but very good at her job; Christina would be the junior *Hoofd Zuster* under Truus and besides that there were four student nurses and several aides.

The Accident Room was vast, modern and magnificently equipped. Christina, having a quick look round before Zuster Bunsma arrived, approved of it all. There was already a sprinkling of patients waiting, but she had no time to investigate what Truus was doing, for Zuster Bunsma had arrived.

She was a large woman with big features, small dark eyes and grey hair, cut very short. She wore no make-up at all and her age could have been anything between fifty and sixty. She wished everyone a good morning in a brisk manner and turned to Christina.

'You come with high recommendations,' she observed without preamble. 'I hope you will prove them right.' She studied Christina slowly. 'You look a sensible young woman; I won't have anyone else in this department.' She added unexpectedly, 'I hope you will be happy working here, Zuster Forbes.' She nodded quickly and went on before Christina could say a word: 'We will go round the department and I will show you everything. You will be expected to remember all I have told you.'

Christina said calmly: 'I shall do my best, Zuster Bunsma,' and was wondering if she had said enough when one of the nurses came to whisper in her superior's ear. Zuster Bunsma frowned. 'You are to go at once to the *Directeur*'s office. This nurse will show you where to go. You will come to me when you return.'

The nurse spoke almost no English, which was

a pity because Christina was dying to find out how it was that Zuster Bunsma's English was so good. She wondered if her Dutch would ever be half as fluent.

Dr ter Brandt had his office on the fourth floor, that much she discovered from her companion, which meant that they had to walk through a number of passages and take the lift. They stopped finally outside a door with his name on it, the nurse tapped and then stood aside with the air of someone who was glad she wasn't the one to be going inside, and Christina walked in.

The room was very large with two tall windows overlooking the courtyard below. It was close-carpeted and had panelled walls and a very large desk, behind which Dr ter Brandt was sitting. He looked up as the door opened and got to his feet.

'Ah, Zuster Forbes, welcome to our hospital.' He came round the desk and shook hands. 'All of us at the Theofilus hope that you will be happy working here.'

'Thank you, I'm sure I shall be, everyone has been very kind. The Accident Room looks splendid…'

'It is also very busy.' He offered her a chair and went to sit behind his desk again. 'You have met Hoofd Zuster Bunsma?'

He was being very formal, she decided, but now of course matters were rather different; she was in his employ. He was treating her with perfect courtesy, but his manner was so impersonal as to seem cold.

'Yes, I have. She was about to show me round when I was told to come here.'

'A splendid nurse, one of the best in the hospital. She has been at the Theofilus for something like thirty years.'

'Before your time,' observed Christina, for the moment forgetting where she was.

His face remained placid, but his eyes gleamed with amusement.

'I am thirty-seven, Christina.'

She had pinkened up to her hair. 'Oh, I do beg your pardon—I quite forgot who you were...'

His eyebrows rose. 'Surely not. It is only a matter of weeks since we last saw each other.'

'I didn't mean that,' she explained, 'what I meant was, I forgot that you're the director. You know, you have to be treated with respect and all that.' She saw him frown and added hastily: 'I've made it worse, but I didn't mean to. Oh, dear I should have been saying sir too. Please excuse me, I suppose I'm excited...'

He gave her a long thoughtful look. 'Ah, yes— Adam will be back in a few days. You must be looking forward to seeing him again.'

The pink which had almost faded returned even

pinker than before. 'Well, yes I hope that is, it would be nice if we met again.'

'I'm sure you will,' his voice was smooth. 'Adam will be here for a few months; he didn't do very well on the course, he'll need more experience.'

'I'm sorry. Perhaps he found it more difficult taking it in London.'

The doctor didn't reply to this. 'If there is anything I can do while you are here, please let me know. You will find the Directrice very kind and understanding, but if at any time you should want to discuss anything with me, please do not hesitate to do so.' He got to his feet and she got out of her chair, bewildered by his change of manner. He opened the door for her and she went past him, making a conventional murmur. Finding her way back to the Accident Room, she supposed she wouldn't see him very often, perhaps never. She was a little surprised to find that the thought depressed her. But only for a moment; Adam would be back very soon now and life would be exciting once more.

And that was the last chance she had to think of him that day. Sister Bunsma was waiting for her when she reached the Accident Room and, mindful of that lady's words, Christina bent all her powers of concentration upon the task of learning as much as she could in the shortest possible time. And when she was released at last, she was told to accompany Truus for the rest of the day, watching her treatment of the various patients, learning if she could, the names of the equipment used and listening all the time. It sounded like nonsense, of course, but she had a quick ear and she was sensible enough to know that once she had got hold of the basic Dutch, she would learn quickly enough.

During the afternoon, she went to her lesson, given by a dry-as-dust elderly man, who without giving her a minute to think, plunged into a list of everyday words which, she heard to her horror, she was expected to repeat word-perfect on the following day. It was a relief to get back to the Accident Room, and because there was a sudden rush on, find herself helping one of the housemen with some uncomplicated arm plasters.

She was tired when she and Truus went off duty at five o'clock but she had enjoyed her day. Not wishing to incur her teacher's wrath on the following afternoon, she refused several friendly offers to go out and made herself comfortable in the sitting room with some of the Sisters and learned her homework, getting a good-natured girl sitting near her to correct her and finally hear her recite it. There was a good deal of friendly laughter over her pronunciation, but she was assured that she was doing remarkably well. She went down to her supper presently, quite pleased with herself.

The next day followed very much the same pattern as the first, only now she was expected to know where most things were kept in the Accident Room and, when it was possible without getting into language difficulties, treat some of the patients. She was elated that her teacher expressed satisfaction at her homework and ploughed her way through a dozen basic sentences, to be told that she was required to be word-perfect on the following day. 'You may think that I am working you hard, young lady,' said her mentor with an unexpected twinkle, 'but you have a natural gift for languages, I think, and if you work hard you should have a good knowledge of our language within three months, perhaps less.'

On the following morning during breakfast she was told to report for duty at once, to find the cubicles occupied with stretchers, dazed people sitting around, and a good deal of noise and bustle. Zuster Bunsma was already there and beckoned her over. 'There is an accident between a touring bus and a car.' She paused to wave two ambulance men towards an empty cubicle. 'Some are not seriously hurt, so far eight are badly injured. It is an English bus, so you will be of great use. Go now to the cubicle in the corner and prepare the patient for examination.' She smiled suddenly. 'Forget that you are in this hospital and think that you are in England. In that way you will work faster.'

There was an elderly woman lying on the couch in the far cubicle. Her face was cut and bleeding and so were her hands, but her extreme pallor might be caused by some more serious damage. Christina said softly: 'Hullo, I've come to get you ready for the doctor. Does anything in particular hurt? I can see your face and hands are cut, we'll see to those, but I must get your shoes and dress off so that we can take a good look.'

'You're English,' mumbled the woman. 'What a blessing! It's my chest, dear such a nasty sharp pain…'

Christina said soothingly: 'Don't worry, Mrs… Burrows, is it? I'll take a quick look, the doctor will be here in a moment.'

There was no injury to be seen; she took the BP, felt for a pulse so faint it was barely perceptible and noted the woman's grey face. A coronary, and the quicker she could get a doctor the better.

She smiled reassuringly at the woman and pressed the alarm buzzer by the side of the couch.

Dr ter Brandt's quiet voice behind her was unexpected, but she didn't waste time on that. She said quietly: 'Mrs Burrows, cuts of face and hands, severe pain in chest, no visible wound there.' She added the startlingly low blood pressure and the almost total absence of pulse, and then raised her voice a little so that the patient could hear her.

'Here's the doctor, Mrs Burrows, you'll be all right now.'

He wasted no time and yet he gave the impression that he was unhurried. Mrs Burrows was examined, sedated and borne away to the Intensive Care Unit in the minimum of time, leaving Christina to clear the cubicle in readiness for the next patient.

Dr ter Brandt had gone within seconds of Mrs Burrows, but before he went he said: 'That was quick thinking, Sister. I congratulate you.'

She was kept busy after that; cuts and concussions, broken bones and shock, but always she was aware that Dr ter Brandt, far from sitting in his office directing, was striding around in a white coat, working twice as hard as anyone else and still looking placid.

Things quietened down slowly. By midday those who needed further treatment had been warded and the rest sent to their hotel. Christina, drinking coffee with Truus while the nurses cleared up, heaved a sigh.

'All those poor souls—what a wretched end to their holiday! What happened to the driver of the car, Truus?'

Truus opened her mouth to tell her and then closed it again, her eyes looking at someone or something over Christina's shoulder. Christina turned round to look too as Dr ter Brandt came further into the office. He spoke to Truus, who got up and went out. 'To fetch me some coffee,' he explained placidly, 'and I cannot think why you should always look so surprised when we meet. Perhaps you will tell me?'

Christina put down her mug. 'Well, you're not at all what I expected.' She said rather crossly because it was difficult to put into words. 'I thought a director would stay in his office...'

His eyes narrowed. 'Indeed? I wonder where you got such a strange idea?' His voice held mockery. 'I have a practice too—but I feel sure that Adam will have told you that already.'

'Yes, he told me that you were the senior partner.'

'Ah, I've disappointed you—naturally you expected someone middle-aged and pompous. Probably going bald...'

If the note of mockery hadn't been there she would have laughed, as it was she said seriously: 'As a matter of fact, I did...'

Truus interrupted her, carrying a tray with fresh coffee, and he sat down on a corner of Zuster Bunsma's desk and drank it.

'I hear you are showing an aptitude for our language.'

How fast the hospital grapevine worked! 'I've only had two lessons.'

He nodded carelessly. 'Mijnheer Beek is a splendid teacher, especially when he has an eager pupil. By the way, you had better ask for a day off on Friday.'

She asked him why, although she had guessed already. A little colour came into her cheeks and her heart doubled its beat.

He started at her with a faint smile which she didn't care for. 'Did you not know? Adam is coming home.' He turned to speak to Truus and bidding them a rather curt goodbye, went away.

Truus collected the mugs and the pair of them went back on duty again.

'He is splendid, the doctor,' said Truus admiringly. Christina agreed absentmindedly, her head deliriously full of Adam.

CHAPTER FOUR

THERE WERE two whole days before Friday, but if she wanted to be free on that day she would have to ask Zuster Bunsma as soon as possible, something Christina wasn't too keen on doing. She had only just arrived and a request for a day off so soon was likely to be frowned upon. If she had been in Zuster Bunsma's place, she would have frowned it down too, and probably Dr ter Brandt had been testing her just to see how keen she was on the job. She went to lunch with Truus, went back for an hour's work in the Accident Room, which she was fast discovering was almost always busy, and then went to her lesson without seeing Zuster Bunsma, still thinking about Adam. So much so that Mijnheer Beek pulled her up quite sharply with the reminder that she would get nowhere at all unless she applied herself to learning at least some of his language. She was sensible enough to see this for herself; for the rest of the hour she was an exemplary pupil.

It was time for their tea break when she got back, but she saw at a glance that they weren't going to get one. The place swarmed with small

children, weeping and howling in concert. Zuster
Bunsma sailed from her office as Christina went
in, with: 'Zuster Forbes, these children were on a
school picnic, and one of them was foolish enough
to stir up a swarm of bees. The stings must be
removed and antihistamine given. You will take
the end cubicle and treat the children in it. There
is a nurse already there.'

It seemed strange, after several years of telling
others what to do, to be given orders oneself. But
logical enough, Christina told herself sensibly as
she made her way to her patients. She was new,
foreign and needed to prove that she could cope
with the job. She pulled back the curtains and
joined the howling mob of little people inside.

It was no good trying to stop them. She didn't
know what to say. She caught a small boy, sat him
down in a chair, gave him a reassuring smile and
a hullo and picked up the dirty little paw, its back
red and swollen.

'Oh, we'll have this out in no time,' she assured
him, and began gently to clean it, talking all the
time. He didn't understand her, of course, but her
voice was soothing and held authority, so he
stopped howling to look at her, and she picked up
the forceps laid ready and whisked out the sting,
handed him over to the nurse for further cleansing
and began on the next child. There were six children in all, although it seemed twice that number,

and she was removing a clutch of nasty stings from the last small leg when Dr ter Brandt came quietly in.

'Last one?' he wanted to know.

'Yes—' she hesitated and added 'sir', and didn't see his grin. 'But I haven't given the antihistamine yet.'

He went across to the trolley and began to draw up the drug, at the same time saying something to the nurse who was with her. The girl went away and he said placidly: 'We should be able to manage this little lot between us—I've told Nurse to help at the other end.'

He was good with children, waiting patiently while Christina caught and held each child, and keeping up an endless stream of talk while he gave the injections so that half the children were screaming their heads off in anticipation of his treatment and the other half were shrieking with laughter.

Finally, with a good deal of giggling and squealing, they were returned to one of the two teachers with them and Christina began to tidy the cubicle, very aware of the doctor sitting on the couch, swinging one leg and watching her. At last, everything done to her satisfaction, she said briskly: 'Thank you for your help, sir. I'll find Zuster Bunsma and see what she would like me to do.'

'Time enough. Did you ask for your day off, Christina?'

Her 'no' was faintly defiant.

'Afraid of the dragon? I imagine not. Ah, I have it—you're new here and you don't think you should ask favours.'

'Something like that,' she answered composedly.

'Very commendable.' His voice was dry. 'But unless you do so you won't be able to see Adam.'

She said with calm: 'It's kind of you to bother yourself about me, Dr ter Brandt, but Adam knows where I am if and when he wants to see me.'

The placid expression on his face didn't alter. He got up from the table, ready to leave. 'You're very sure of yourself, and of Adam. I wonder? He favours pretty girls, you know, and you aren't pretty, Christina.' With which outspoken remark he went away, leaving her white-faced with fury.

She spent the rest of the day thinking up stinging remarks to make to him when they met, only they didn't. And the next morning, going on duty, when she met him in a corridor, unfamiliar in slacks and a sweater, she had been surprised enough to answer his good morning with no trace of coldness. 'There has been much business,' observed Truus, hurrying to catch her up. 'A fire and people injured.'

'Is that why he's up?' asked Christina.

'Naturally Dr ter Brandt is there when there is work,' said Truus a little coldly.

Christina ignored the coldness. 'Does he live here, then?'

'No, no. He lives at Scheveningen. There he has a practice in—how do you say?—rooms...'

'Consulting rooms,' supplied Christina.

'That is so. Also he has a house there.'

Even though she disliked him so much there was no reason why she shouldn't know something about him. There were several questions on the tip of her tongue, but they were already going through the door into the Accident Room, and it was, she saw at a glance, a hive of activity.

It was astonishing the number of people who damaged themselves on the way to work in the morning. Christina, examining the cut hand of a girl who had fallen over clutching a milk bottle, forgot all about Dr ter Brandt, forgot about being angry and just a little anxious in case Adam had forgotten her completely, forgot that she was twenty-seven, and on the best authority not a pretty girl; she became absorbed in her work and the busy day ahead of her.

She didn't know whether she was pleased or not when she saw the off duty book later that day. She had her day off and the day following it too. But it was impossible to tell whether it had been Zuster Bunsma's own idea or whether Dr ter Brandt had arranged it. In any case, she had heard nothing from Adam. She went to bed that night feeling despondent and looked the next morning at the post pigeonholed for the nursing staff. There was nothing for her.

She was kept too busy to brood over it during the day. She had found her feet by now and after three lessons was in possession of a handful of useful Dutch words. Besides, she had an ear for languages; unable to understand most of what was said around her, she could still guess the gist of it, and Truus or Zuster Bunsma were never far away. She was left quite often now to carry out the Casualty Officer's instructions and the patients, once they grasped the fact that she knew what she was doing, weren't unduly disturbed. She went off duty a good deal later than usual because there had been a sudden rush of patients in the late afternoon and she had offered to stay on. As she pointed out to Zuster Bunsma, she wasn't doing anything that evening and she was free to lie in bed in the morning if she wanted to.

So it was almost time for first supper as she left the Accident Room and began the walk through the hospital which would bring her to the lift taking her to the top floor and her room. As she went she wondered how she would spend her free time. Adam, she decided sadly, wasn't going to telephone or write; probably he had scores of interesting friends to visit. She would turn herself into a tourist—there was a tremendous amount to see; the Ridderzaal, the Mauritshuis, the Costume Museum and the Royal Library. They would do for a start, and as for a meal, Truus had told her to go to de Bijenkorf, a big department store in the centre of den Haag, or if she was short of cash, there was a good snack bar in Hema, which as far as she could make out was a mixture of Woolworth's and British Home Stores.

She was almost at the lift when she paused. Perhaps there was a letter for her; it wouldn't take a minute to retrace her steps and look. She was half way there even while she was thinking it.

There was nothing. She stood looking at the empty compartment for a moment and then turned round. She had been silly to come, she told herself.

Adam was behind her; she almost fell against him and he flung his arms around her, laughing at her surprised face. And not just surprised, it glowed with sudden delight, her grey eyes sparkled and her mouth curved into a wide smile. 'Adam!' she cried in a small breathless voice. 'Adam!'

He kissed her lightly. 'Hullo, Chrissy. Are you glad to see me?' and then, 'Lord I'd forgotten what glorious eyes you have.'

'Oh, Adam, it's lovely to see you again!'

'So you did miss me.' He looked down at her

with a smile to charm the heart out of her, which became a little mocking as he stared at her.

'You look very severe in that outfit, and years older than you are. For heaven's sake, why have you dragged your hair back like that, and your nose is shining…'

She was too happy to mind. 'I'm only just off duty and we've been busy.' She remembered where they were and looked round the entrance hall; there was no one there and she was conscious of relief. Dr ter Brandt, she felt sure, wouldn't approve of Adam's arm round her.

'Well, go and pretty yourself up, we're going out for a meal.' He put his other arm round her and bent to kiss her once more.

'Not here,' Dr ter Brandt's voice sounded weary, or bored or both. 'Adam, I must ask you to remember where you are.'

He had come in through the swing doors of the hospital and was standing looking at them with an expressionless face. After a moment he continued on his way with a polite, 'Good evening, Christina,' as he went.

She murmured, 'Good evening, sir,' her face red, but Adam didn't look in the least put out. His brother had barely disappeared when he said, half laughing, 'Good lord, darling, you don't call Duert sir, do you?'

'Yes, of course I do. I'm working for him and

he's the director.' She raised troubled eyes to his. 'I wish he hadn't seen us, Adam.'

He shrugged his shoulders. 'Surely you don't mind? He's a good chap, but he's got out-of-date ideas. He's not above kissing a girl himself, but only in the right place, certainly not here.' He laughed. 'We must get him to change his views, mustn't we? Now do go and change, there's a dear girl—I'm famished.' And when she still hesitated: 'Don't let him worry you, for heaven's sake, Chrissy—he won't dismiss you; as long as you do your work well and we're discreet, he won't be in the least interested.'

She went then, her pleasure at going out with Adam tempered with a strong wish that Dr ter Brandt hadn't arrived just when he did. He must think her a cheap sort of young woman; he had wished her a very civil good evening, but his eyes had swept over her as though she hadn't been there.

She showered and changed into the green jersey dress and a velvet blazer and took care to do her hair in the new style she hadn't bothered with since she had come to Holland. It was disappointing to be greeted with Adam's: 'There you are. You've worn that dress before.' He saw the look on her face and added: 'Its pretty, that's why I remember it.'

His smile stilled the small stab of uncertainty.

'I'm glad you like it.' She kept her voice calm with an effort because just to be with him again was so wonderful.

He took her to the restaurant at the end of the pier at Scheveningen, driving his car with a reckless speed with rather took her breath, and parking it on the boulevard before walking her along the pier. The restaurant was attractive and the food good, although Christina hardly noticed what she was eating. Adam had set out to charm her and was succeeding; she had always been possessed of a sound common sense, now she had none. She listened to his outrageous flattery and believed it because she wanted to, and when he embarked on plans for their future amusement she agreed to them all. He was to work at the Theofilus, he told her, getting experience in both surgery and medicine, and when she asked him eagerly for how long he grinned disarmingly at her and told her for as long as she wanted him to. The evening flew by, and at the end of it she bade him goodnight rather primly, mindful of his brother's capacity for turning up unexpectedly. But the entrance hall was empty and quiet, only the faint murmur and quiet footsteps of the night staff and the squeaking of an occasional trolley emphasised the stillness. Christina went soft-footed to the lift, gained her room and went dreamily to bed. She woke in the night, blindingly aware that she was behaving like a schoolgirl in love for the first time. But what did that matter if Adam loved her too?

He was taking her out to lunch the next day. She got up late, dressed with care, with the resolve to get some new clothes with her first pay packet and went out of one of the side doors to where his car was parked. She had to wait a little while and when he came, ten minutes later, he was carelessly apologetic. 'Duert kept me,' he told her, 'wanted to talk about my future. I told him I was happy enough with the present.'

He opened the car door and she got in as he settled himself beside her.

'Are you free too?' she asked him.

'Good lord, no. I'm supposed to be going to do a round with Dr van Tripp at two o'clock.'

Christina searched her memory. 'The senior physician? So you like medicine?'

Adam belted along the road in the direction of Scheveningen. 'Can't stand it, but Duert says I must do six months with van Tripp. I don't intend to, of course.'

'What will you do then?'

He said airily: 'No idea—surgery, I suppose. I need a holiday—Duert seems to think I'm a man of iron as he is. Always got his nose to the grindstone, poor chap—a pity he didn't marry.'

'Well, there's nothing to stop him, is there?'

'Oh, yes there is—unrequited love, darling. He

fell in love years ago with a girl—a beautiful dolly who threw him over for a millionaire. Duert's rich, but he's not that rich.'

She felt a pang of pity. 'Oh, the poor man! I'm sorry.'

Adam chuckled. 'Don't waste your pity on him, Chrissy, he's able to take care of himself.'

They were in Scheveningen now, going down the Badhuisweg. 'I thought we'd eat a *nasi goreng* at the Bali.' He glanced at his watch. 'No time to talk much, I'm afraid, but we can meet again later.'

They ate their meal a little hurriedly and Adam left her without ceremony at the end of it. 'You'll enjoy looking round the shops,' he told her airily, 'and there are trams to take you back when you feel like it. I'd drive you back, but I mustn't upset old Duert by being late for van Tripp's round.'

Christina was left standing outside the restaurant, feeling at a loss, but making excuses for Adam. It had been sweet of him to take her out to lunch when he had so short a time in which to do it, and he was quite right, she would enjoy looking at the shops. She ignored the small nagging thought at the back of her mind; that Adam held his brother in wholesome awe even though he derided him so wittily, and there had really been no reason why he shouldn't have driven her back with him.

She spent a pleasant enough afternoon, admiring

the expensive clothes and trifles in the shop windows, deciding what she would buy when she had some money and having tea at an elegant little tearoom. The bill staggered her when she saw it; she would have done better to have gone back to den Haag and found Hema. She boarded a tram presently and went back into the city because the shops were shut now and she had nowhere else to go. Then she went back to the Theofilus and, much to her discomfiture, came face to face with Dr ter Brandt as she crossed the courtyard.

His 'Good evening, Christina,' was deliberately spoken, and just as deliberate was his pause as he reached her. Short of ducking round him she couldn't avoid him, so she said, 'Good evening, sir,' with something of a snap and a decidedly heightened colour.

He didn't seem to notice either. 'You have no need to call me sir when you are off duty,' he told her mildly. 'I hope you enjoyed your day with Adam?'

She frowned a little. 'Well, it wasn't a day, actually. He took me to lunch, but he had to get back to do a round with Dr van Tripp.'

Her companion's face didn't alter its placid expression, but his eyes beneath half-closed lids were suddenly alert. 'Ah, yes,' he said smoothly, 'I'd forgotten that, but there is still this evening.'

'You've forgotten that you recommended him to

attend that lecture at the…' she frowned again, 'I've forgotten the name, but it's at Leiden.'

He said unsmilingly: 'I become increasingly forgetful. The place you mention is the University, close to the Hortus Botanicus gardens. Leiden is a charming place, you must visit it some time.'

He didn't seem to expect an answer and she couldn't think of one anyway. After a little pause she said awkwardly: 'Goodbye, Dr ter Brandt I expect you're on your way home.' For answer he caught her gently by the elbow, turned her round and walked her back the way she had come. 'No,' he said pleasantly, 'I have someone to see presently. I came out merely for a breath of air and a cup of coffee. Perhaps you will join me? I should like to hear what you think of den Haag and the hospital. First impressions are always interesting.' And when she didn't answer at once: 'Unless you have other plans?'

'No, I haven't,' said Christina baldly.

'Splendid. You don't mind if we walk?'

'No—no, of course not.'

They crossed the busy street and plunged into a succession of small streets and narrow lanes, coming out surprisingly quickly into Langue Voorhout where the doctor turned almost immediately into a small restaurant. Christina just had time to read the name—Le Bistroquet—as they went inside.

It was small and, she judged, expensive, and

hardly the place in which to drink coffee. Even as she thought it Dr ter Brandt murmured, 'I missed lunch—would it be asking too much of you to join me in a meal?' And at her look of enquiry: 'Yes, I know I could eat at the Hospital, but as we are here…?' His raised brows asked her a question.

'Thank you,' she said composedly, 'I should like to.'

Which was true enough. Since she couldn't dine with Adam, anyone or anything would do to help her pass her solitary evening. Besides, she didn't particularly want to go to supper at the hospital.

The doctor appeared to be well known. She accepted a drink and studied the menu, secretly appalled at the prices. She searched for the cheaper dishes, reading the French carefully, unaware of her companion's eyes upon her face. When she said that she'd have an omelette fines herbes and nothing else, his firm mouth curved into a faint smile.

'Oh, you must have more than that,' he begged her. 'I'm famished, but I can't eat while you nibble at a snack. How about avocado vinaigrette, sole Véronique and one of their hot soufflés? I'm sure Adam gave you a splendid lunch, but you must have some sort of an appetite by now.'

His voice was casual, but his eyes were intent.

'Oh, yes—it was lovely.' She sounded forlorn without knowing it.

'The forerunner of many more, I daresay,' he observed easily. 'And now, tell me what you think of the Theofilus.'

Christina was surprised, thinking about it afterwards, to find that she had enjoyed her evening. Dr ter Brandt had been amusing, pleasant and a good host. She was quite sure she didn't like him, but that was largely because he had Adam under his thumb. Poor Adam, she thought as she brushed her hair and got ready for bed, having to spend his evening at some stuffy lecture.

She went to sleep almost at once, happily unaware that Dr ter Brandt, having returned to the hospital with her, was waiting patiently in his office for his brother. He had to wait quite a while and when at last Adam was ushered in he wasted no time.

'I should like to know why you missed the teaching round this afternoon, Adam, and why you saw fit to lie to Christina?' He sat back in his chair and studied his brother through half-shut lids. 'I seem to remember telling you that Christina wasn't quite the same as your usual girl-friends. I suggest that you leave her alone.'

Adam scowled. 'Look here, I took the girl out to lunch, that's all. I can't help it if she's got some silly ideas into her head, can I?' The scowl changed into an ingratiating smile. 'Look, Duert, I just want to give Christina a bit of fun. Once she's found her feet and made some friends, she'll forget all about me.' His eyes narrowed. 'Not keen on her yourself, are you?' and then at the cold stare he got, added hastily: 'All right, I was only joking!'

His brother remained silent and Adam rattled on: 'Tell you what—I'll take her to the Annual Ball and introduce her to as many people as I can. You surely won't object to that?'

'No, provided that Christina wishes to go. And now you're here, Adam, be good enough to take your job seriously, or there'll be trouble.'

Adam, with a lighthearted goodnight, strolled off, leaving Duert sitting behind his desk, staring at the writing pad on it with a thoughtful look.

Christina didn't get up until everyone along the corridor had gone on duty. There was no hurry, the day was before her and she had nothing to do. She bathed and dressed slowly, made herself coffee in the tiny kitchenette near her room, and prepared to go out. It was a pleasant enough morning, the pale, wide sky with small clouds scudding across it before the wind, hinted at rain later, but as she had the half-formed plan to spend most of her day in museums and the larger shops, that wouldn't matter. It was a pity that Truus was on duty all day, otherwise they might have spent the afternoon together. She was already on good terms with several of the Sisters, but most of them went home for their days off and those that didn't were on duty.

She gained the entrance hall, wished the porter in his little box good morning and made for the entrance, glancing at the post in its pigeonholes as she went.

There was quite a pile under F and the porter, seeing her stop, went to look through it. Two letters, one from George Henry, and the other unstamped, her name scrawled right across the envelope.

She put her brother's letter in her pocket; she could read that presently, over a cup of coffee. The second envelope she tore open eagerly; she felt sure it was from Adam, and she was right.

His writing was large and flourishing so that what was really only a brief note seemed like a long letter covering two pages. He was free that afternoon, he told her, and would take her out to tea. Would she be at the Pier Restaurant again at half past three? He was hers, Adam.

Of course she would be there. She didn't pause to wonder what would happen if she refused, nor did it enter her head that he was taking her very much for granted. She wandered out into the watery sunshine with a head full of dreams.

But half past three was a long way off. She found her way to the Mauritshuis and, once there, forgot all the other places she intended visiting. She left it two hours later, her head a happy jumble of Old Masters, and had her coffee at a snack bar while she read George Henry's letter. He was happy and relieved that she had settled in so well. The wedding was to be the following week and Hilary sent her love. Christina made a mental note that she must get a card to send, and then, because it was already noon, had another cup of coffee and a *kaas broodje* with it.

Refreshed, she set out for the shops, lingering from one window to the next. It was a pity that a sudden downpour left her bedraggled and damp, but by then there was no time to do more than smooth her skirt and run a comb through her hair. If she was to reach Scheveningen by half past three, she would have to hurry.

Adam was waiting for her and her glow of delight at seeing him was a little chilled by his sudden frown. 'Didn't you have an umbrella?' he asked after a perfunctory greeting.

'It was dry when I came out this morning,' she reminded him. 'Do I look awful?'

There wasn't much make-up left on her face and her hair was less than perfect, but her grey eyes were lovely. 'You look gorgeous, darling—you always do.'

Adam uttered the compliment with the smoothness of much practice, caught her arm and hurried her into the restaurant. Sitting at a table overlooking the sea, her make-up repaired and her hair redone, she smiled at him happily. 'Have you a half day?' she asked.

'Not quite—that would be too generous of Duert. I'm on duty again at six o'clock, but I wanted to see you. Has anybody told you about the Annual Ball?' he added. 'Well, you've hardly been here long enough, I suppose. It's held at the Theofilus in two weeks' time. Will you come with me? It's great fun. Of course, you'll have to do something about your hair and you'll need a decent dress. I know several girls who'll love to take you round the shops.' He put out a hand and covered hers with it. 'Say you'll come, otherwise I won't go.'

Common sense told her to ignore that; of course he'd go whether she was there or not, but it was nice to hear him say it. 'I'd like to come with you,' she told him, careful not to sound too excited. 'I'd rather buy my own dress, though, if you don't mind, and I'll find a good hairdresser.'

'Splendid!' Adam took the tea she had poured out and began an amusing account of his morning's work. He didn't take his work very seriously, but she had no doubt that he was clever at it. He was already a junior partner with his brother, although there were two other doctors who shared the practice as well. Christina would have liked to have known where his home was, although he had to live in at the hospital. Somewhere close by, pre-

sumably, since Dr ter Brandt spent a good deal of
his day at the Theofilus, but she couldn't quite
bring herself to ask Adam. It was a funny thing,
but although she was so hopelessly infatuated with
him she wasn't quite sure of him as a friend. She
thought with surprise that she had told Dr ter
Brandt a whole lot of things she would never tell
Adam—he would have been bored. She wondered
what miracle had caused him to single her out from
all the much prettier girls he must know. One day
she would ask him.

They walked along the boulevard when they had
had their tea. The rain had stopped, but grey clouds
were piling up over the cold looking sea. Christina
found it exhilarating and urged Adam to take her
to the far end where the fishing harbours were. But
when she would have stayed to look at the moored
fishing boats and all the paraphernalia that went
with them, he showed signs of impatience. It didn't
matter, she told herself, she could come again on
her own or with one of the Sisters, and next time
she would walk along the promenade or even along
the firm sand at the water's edge.

Now she was content to remain almost silent
while Adam talked—he was an amusing talker and
she listened with pleasure to his racy comments
about people he knew, but it was over too soon.
Presently he drove her back to the hospital and this
time there was no Dr ter Brandt to invite her to

drink coffee with him. Not that she minded; she didn't give it a thought, she was glad to find the Sisters' sitting room empty, so that she could mull over her afternoon and everything Adam had said, and dwell happily on the prospect of going to the dance with him. She was so deeply engrossed in thinking up a suitable outfit for this event that she almost missed her supper.

CHAPTER FIVE

CHRISTINA HEARD all about the dance at breakfast the next morning. Someone mentioned it and at once there was a burst of talk, laboriously translated for her benefit. Everyone was going, as far as she could make out, and when one of the girls at the table suggested kindly that a partner must be found for her, and she told them briefly that she had been invited to go by Adam ter Brandt, there was a sudden silence, instantly covered up by an outburst of talk. The talk was so animated that she fancied that she must have imagined the tiny pause, and she quickly forgot it in the ensuing discussion about clothes. One dressed, it seemed, in one's very best. The *burgermeester*, a sprinkling of foreign consuls and all the upper crust of den Haag society would be there. 'Beautiful dresses, jewels,' declared Leenie dramatically. 'We do not, how do you say? compete, but we look nice.' She beamed at Christina. 'You have a dress?'

'No,' said Christina, 'I haven't—I thought I'd get something...'

'Blue,' observed Truus, and was instantly contradicted by half a dozen voices. All the colours of the rainbow were suggested, but Christina laughed and shook her head. 'It'll be a secret,' she told them.

And there the matter rested. The Accident Room was as usual bursting with patients all the morning, and in the afternoon, when there was a lull, she had her lesson. She rather enjoyed it because she persuaded her sober teacher to instruct her on how to buy clothes.

She was on the point of going off duty when she heard the ambulances clamour. She had turned back to join Zuster Bunsma before it had stopped at the wide doors, and was surprised when that lady said abruptly: 'You are off duty, Zuster Forbes.'

'Yes, I know,' said Christina, 'but Zuster Felman has just gone to X-Ray for you and Zuster Keizer's busy with that fractured clavicle.'

Zuster Bunsma shot her a look and then nodded. 'I shall be glad of help.'

She had never spoken a truer word. The first ambulance, containing two young men who had been hit about the head with a blunt instrument, was followed by a second and a third. The policeman who roared up on a motorbike had a short discussion with one of the Casualty Officers, who told Zuster Bunsma, who in turn found time to tell Christina.

'A gang fight,' she said in her fluent, accented

English, 'wild boys who will perhaps make difficulties here. You do not feel frightened?'

'No—at least, I haven't so far.'

'I have asked for male nurses—Zuster Keizer and Zuster Felman are young and pretty, so they can go to one of the wards.'

Zuster Bunsma sailed away to cope with a belligerent youth with a cut head, leaving Christina to wonder if she really was as plain and elderly as that lady had implied.

Most of the patients were quiet enough, anyway. They must have had frightful headaches, judging from the cuts and bruises, but a handful of them were proving difficult to manage. Christina, doing her best to make a gangling youth sit down while she cleaned up a nasty knife wound on his check, was taken off guard when he put up a hand and caught her wrist, twisting it painfully. He laughed when she said, 'Let go,' not understanding her, and she struggled to think of a suitable phrase from one of her lessons which might suit the occasion. There wasn't any; she had been taught to ask for the salt, enquire the time, ask if there was pain, was there a headache and a dozen other useful sentences, but none of them met her requirements. She gave her wrist a sharp tug and winced with the pain. Her other hand still held a swab firmly to his cheek, she would have to drop it and slap his face or would that be assault? She said calmly: 'You really are a silly twit,' then dropped the swab as a large hand grasped her shoulder.

'Trouble, Christina?' enquired Dr ter Brandt in a mild voice. The mildness was only for her, though. She had no idea what he said to her patient, in a cold abrupt voice which caused him to drop her wrist as though it were a hot coal, but it was instantly effective. The boy remained silent and unmoving while she cleaned the wound and then held his head steady while the doctor stitched the cut under a local anaesthetic, and when he had been handed over to one of the waiting policemen, Christina began clearing the trolley. There was another ambulance coming and everyone else had their hands full at the moment. She wondered what it would be this time and was startled when the doctor lifted her hand from the couch she was changing and examined her wrist.

'You'll have a bruise, I'm afraid. I'll take a look at it later. We'll have whatever this is in here, please.'

So Christina went to meet the ambulance men with the stretcher with: '*Hier, alstublieft,*' and watched while they deposited their burden on her newly cleaned couch.

Quite a different kettle of fish; a not so young woman, poorly dressed and grubby. Christina had taken a quick look at her and said urgently: 'Shall we get her to Maternity at once, sir?'

'No, I don't think there's time. Get some clothes off her and I'll scrub.' He said something to one of the ambulance men and went across to one of the telephones. 'I've asked Maternity to send down a couple of nurses and a stretcher.'

The woman opened her eyes for a moment. 'You're English!' Two tears trickled down her cheeks. 'It's like a miracle!'

Christina was peeling off clothes and arranging blankets. 'Yes, dear—they do happen. Could you tell us your name—and should we tell anyone? Your husband?' She glanced at the wedding ring on the woman's finger.

The woman sounded hopeless. 'He's gone. He worked here and when he sent for me I came to Holland, but they told me that he'd gone to some-where or other—the Middle East—he works on those oil rigs.'

'No one else?' enquired Christina softly.

'No,' she sighed. 'The name's Brown, Liz Brown.'

Christina stood aside as Dr ter Brandt bent over his patient. 'This isn't your first?'

Mrs Brown had shut her eyes again. 'No, doc-tor—I've two more. They're with my sister in Not-tingham.'

'You hadn't the money to get home?' It was more a statement than a question.

'That's right.' Her voice came out on a sigh. 'Can't believe my luck coming here.'

Dr ter Brandt glanced across at Christina. 'Got the blanket ready?' he wanted to know, and then to his patient, 'Everything will be all right now, Mrs Brown, you and the baby will be in bed in no time at all.'

Which was quite true. Ten minutes later Mrs Brown was studying the small bundle in her arms. 'I always wanted a daughter,' she said, and fell instantly asleep.

Dr ter Brandt was giving instructions to the nurse who had come down from Maternity, and presently Mrs Brown and the baby were whisked away. Christina, clearing up yet again, asked in a troubled voice: 'What will happen to her? The poor soul!'

'We'll keep her in for a couple of weeks, get her on her feet again and in the meantime I'll see what I can do to get her back home. We might even trace her husband.'

'The villain!' said Christina with feeling, and then: 'Do you always come down to the Accident Room when there's a rush on, sir?'

'If I'm free. Are you disappointed to find that I don't spend the day behind my desk?'

'No—oh, no.' She spoke too quickly because somehow Adam had given the impression that was just what his elder brother did do. She added: 'You can't have much time at home.'

He didn't answer and she went pink; he had every right to snub, of course, she had been too inquisitive. It was a relief when there was a sudden influx of patients and Zuster Bunsma called her to take over a small snivelling girl who had been bitten by a dog. By the time the small creature had been dealt with, there was no sign of the doctor. Back in his office, presumably. Christina cleared up and longed for her supper. Probably she wouldn't get any, it was long past the time for that meal, the night staff already on duty. She supposed she would have to go out to one of the snack bars close to the hospital and get coffee and something to eat. Perhaps one of the other girls would go with her. Adam was away, so there was no hope of seeing him. Christina said goodnight to Zuster Bunsma and started off in the direction of the canteen; there was a chance that it might still be open. It wasn't, and she was retracing her footsteps when she met Zuster Bunsma again.

'I am looking for you, Zuster Forbes,' said that lady at once. 'Dr ter Brandt wishes to see your wrist—it was injured this evening, is it not so? Kindly to come with me.'

Christina thinking longingly of food, went meekly enough. Zuster Bunsma wasn't the kind of person one argued with.

She was led to Women's Surgical, where she found Leenie, still on duty and talking to Dr ter Brandt in her little office. Christina, feeling rather a fool, paused in the doorway and he looked up to say: 'Ah, yes, I think I should take a look at your wrist, Zuster Forbes—hospital rules, you know. You have had your supper?'

She felt like telling him that since he seemed to have a finger in everyone's pie, why Women's Surgical at nine o'clock in the evening? Surely there were surgical housemen on duty? he must know she had missed that meal. She said stonily: 'The canteen is closed, but I intended going out for a meal, thank you, sir. I was on my way…'

His blue eyes held hers for a brief moment. He said something to Leenie and then came over to Christina, picked up her hand and examined her wrist. There was an ugly bruise already and it was painful, but that was all; she said so in a matter-of-fact voice and he agreed with her coolly enough, adding: 'If you will go with Zuster Bunsma, she will see that you have your supper.'

It was on the tip of her tongue to refuse, but something in his face stopped her. She said. 'Very well, sir,' and added a quiet goodnight as she followed the older woman out of the office.

The canteen door, which had been shut, was now open. Zuster Bunsma sailed through it and sat down at one of the smaller tables, waving to Christina to sit down too. The supper they were served was excellent and her companion, unbending now that she was off duty, proved to be entertaining and informative, only she wasn't informative about Dr ter Brandt. The discreet questions Christina put about him were ignored. Of course, she told herself, getting ready for bed later, Adam had told her a good deal about his brother, but always jokingly—that tale about unrequited love, for instance. She got into bed and lay wondering about that. Somehow the doctor didn't give the impression of being a man with a broken heart; on the other hand, his manner gave nothing away—that annoying placid expression... She went to sleep.

She sensed a subtle difference in Zuster Bunsma's manner towards her after that particular evening. She was left to get on with it now, floundering about in her sparse Dutch but on the whole coping very well. Injuries were the same all over the world, a broken leg was a broken leg whatever it was called, during the next few days she increased her vocabulary, not bothering with long sentences; learning essential words as fast as she could, greatly encouraged by her teacher who had the sense not to bother her with too much grammar.

She was beginning to enjoy her job and she would have been quite happy if she could have seen more of Adam. But he, his days filled with work on the wards, had no time to do more than send her scribbled notes. They all began 'Darling' and ended 'your Adam', and Christina cherished them, reading them over and over again, and although she was much too busy to think about him during her busy days, she allowed her sensible head to be filled by daydreams during her leisure. Not that she had much of that; she had made friends quickly enough, and if it wasn't Leenie or Truus taking her on a tour of den Haag, one of the other Sisters would take their place. Christina learnt a great deal about the city during the ensuing days, but when one morning she met Adam in the hospital and he told her that they would be going to the ball in a week's time, she cried off accompanying anyone for a day or two, explaining that she wanted to buy a dress, promising that if she got into difficulties she would ask for their help.

So, armed with her dictionary and a great deal of good-natured advice from her friends, Christina made her way to the shopping centre.

She hadn't a great deal of money, but what she had she was well prepared to spend. It didn't take her long to discover that the big stores were beyond her purse, and the cheaper, popular shops had nothing quite right for the occasion. She took to the arcades and small side streets, and in one of the boutiques found what she sought. It was a simple dress, well made and a perfect fit, its grey chiffon cleverly cut to fall in folds over a silk slip. She bought it, although it left her purse almost empty, but she was quite reckless by now. Pay day wasn't far off and she need spend no more money until then; there was just enough for a pair of evening shoes if she could find them. It seemed a hopeless task. There were gold and silver sandals in abundance but none in pale grey satin. By a stroke of luck, just as she was about to give up the search, she found a pair of white satin sandals, shop-soiled and therefore cheap. She bought them and, after some difficulty with the language, bought a pale grey dye.

It was on her way back that she realised that she hadn't enough money to go to a hairdresser. She would have to do the best she could with Truus's electric rollers…

The dying was fairly successful. Christina eyed the faint streaks with some misgivings and made a mental note not to let her feet be seen more than was absolutely necessary. She tried the dress on that evening before an admiring audience, who agreed that it was just right. 'Although jewels would be nice,' observed Leenie, 'pearls or gold chains…'

'Silver!' exclaimed Christina. 'I've got two.' They were produced and put on and declared to be perfect.

'And now your hair,' said Truus. 'We will have a *repetitie*.'

'A what?' Christina thumbed through her dictionary. 'Oh, a rehearsal.'

She sat patiently while several pairs of hands wound her hair round the rollers and presently unwound it. It was Truus who brushed it out, letting it hang almost to her shoulders and then brushing the ends up into a thick bouncy roll. Christina, studying the result, was taken aback. She looked younger and less ordinary; all the same it didn't seem quite her. But it was a change. She turned to Truus to thank her, but that young lady already had the brush in her hand once more. 'I am wrong,' she cried, 'it must be others...' She went to a drawer and rummaged around and came back with a narrow velvet ribbon. 'This,' she said. 'You will sit still, Christina.'

She tied the ribbon round Christina's head and then rolled her hair round it, brushing the front high and letting it wave softly round her face. The result was entirely satisfactory. It might lack the sophisticated elegance of a hairdresser, but it suited her. Highly delighted with themselves, her friends took themselves off to their respective rooms and Christina hung her finery away and brushed out her hair. She hoped with all her heart that Adam would find her appearance even half as nice as her friends had done.

She had brief glimpses of him during the next few days and on one evening he took her to Scheveningen for a drink after they had come off duty, declaring that he had missed her beyond anything and that Duert was working him far too hard. 'It's all very well for him, sitting behind a desk all day', he declared. 'He's forgotten what it's like to be young.'

Christina made the mistake of disagreeing with him. 'Well, he doesn't sit behind a desk all day,' she pointed out reasonably. 'He came down to the Accident Room last week and worked as hard as the rest of us. I don't know how he manages a practice as well as the hospital.'

'Oh, he lives for his work,' said Adam sulkily. 'I told you he hasn't any use for women; he's not the marrying kind. I daresay it would have been all right with that first girl.'

Christina hoped that he would go on, but disappointingly, he didn't.

She saw very little of Duert ter Brandt and only once to speak to. He was standing outside the Surgical Ward entrance as she was passing, talking to two housemen, but he paused when he saw her, and with a word to them deliberately stopped her.

'Good morning, Christina,' his voice was as placid as his face. 'Are you going to the Ball with Adam?'

She forgot to say good morning. 'Yes, yes, I am.'

He stood towering over her, staring down at her. His, 'Good, good,' was casual and after a moment, a little bewildered, she inched away. 'Don't let me keep you,' he begged her, leaving her to wonder why he had stopped her in the first place. She was left with the feeling that she had been dismissed from his mind absolutely, but there was so much more to think about that she thought no more about it.

She was working hard at her lessons now and making progress, and she was enjoying her work too. Answering Hilary's rather acid letters, she was able to say with perfect truth that she had never been so contented with her lot. And there were the preparations for the ball to fill her spare time. She had practised her new hair-style under Truus's friendly eye and there was a constant coming and going between rooms to admire dresses and borrow things.

The ball was to be held in the lecture hall at the back of the hospital and Christina was to meet Adam in the foyer there. She dressed slowly, made up her face with anxious care and started on her hair. It went up like a dream. Truus, coming to make sure that she had got it right, was delighted.

'And the dress is pretty,' she declared. 'You look nice.'

'And so do you,' said Christina. 'But you're so pale, Truus. Don't you feel well?'

Truus made a face. 'I have eaten something that is not good, I think. It will pass.'

Several Sisters went through the hospital together and Christina with them. She looked calm and serene, but her insides were in a terrible turmoil. Suppose Adam wasn't there?

But he was, looking rather impatient, but perhaps that was a good sign. She chose to think so, and then felt suddenly apprehensive because the dresses around her were so lovely, making the grey chiffon which had looked so right and elegant in the boutique quite insignificant. Adam's 'There you are, you look like a mouse,' didn't do much to raise her self-confidence either, but he smiled at her with such charm that she decided that he had meant it as a compliment and beamed at him with delight.

'Isn't it super?' she demanded of him. 'And everyone looks so marvellous.'

He laughed and squeezed her hand. 'What a kid you are! I think it's all a bit of a bore, but it's been done for years and Duert is the last one to go against tradition.'

'Does he think it's a bore too?'

He shrugged. 'I haven't any idea, but even if he did, he would never allow anyone to know. Let's go in.'

The lecture hall had been lavishly decorated with flowers and blazed with lights and up at the other end a band was playing to a floor already nicely full. There was a group of people standing just inside the big double doors—the Directrice, almost unrecognisable in plum velvet, a rather stout lady in mauve brocade, a distinguished-looking elderly man wearing a heavy gold chain over his evening dress, and Duert ter Brandt. Christina thought he looked magnificent in his white tie and tails, completely at ease, bending a little to listen to something the Directrice was saying.

'This is all a bit silly,' muttered Adam as they paused to shake hands, first with Duert and the Directrice and then with the Burgermeester and his lady, but Christina found it rather nice to be treated as a guest and greeted as such. She smiled rather shyly at the Directrice, and was passed to the doctor and was disappointed to be given a pleasant and quite impersonal greeting, for all the world as if he wanted to get it over with as quickly as possible. She flushed a little as he introduced her to the Burgermeester and his wife. Perhaps he hadn't approved of her going with Adam. But when he had asked her whether she was going to be at the Ball with Adam and she had said yes, he had said, 'Good, good,' in rather a strange way. She pulled her wandering wits together and replied to the Burgermeester's carefully spoken Dutch with her painstakingly learned conventional sentences, appreciating the compliment he was paying her. He could just as easily have addressed her in English, she was sure of that.

The band was playing a conventional foxtrot and she and Adam took to the floor at once. 'It's a bit staid to start with,' he told her. 'When the Burgermeester goes, we let go a bit.' He added with surprise, 'I say, you dance well.'

Christina glowed at his praise. She wasn't all that good, actually, but she was light on her feet and quick to respond. They circled the hall, while Adam greeted his friends, pausing every now and then to speak to one or other of them. Some of the girls were lovely and he appeared to be on excellent terms with them. 'I shall have to dance with one or two girls presently,' he told her, and made a funny face at her. 'Distant cousins and daughters of members of the Hospital Board.' He sounded as though he disliked the idea. 'I'll introduce you to a couple of chaps—they'll look after you until I get back.'

Of course he had to circulate, she told herself sensibly. He must know almost everyone who was there, and there weren't only hospital staff, there were dignitaries from den Haag, a sprinkling of officials from the Consulates and all the local doctors and their wives, so she agreed cheerfully

enough, and presently when there was a pause in
the dancing she was introduced to a group of girls
and young men. The group changed every few
minutes as couples left it to dance or joined it, and
presently one of the men, a houseman on the medical side, asked her to dance. When they rejoined
his friends there was no sign of Adam. The second
man Adam had introduced her to swung her on to
the floor before she had time to look around her.
He wasn't dancing as far as she could see, but his
brother was, with an exquisitely turned out young
woman who was laughing a lot as he talked. Christina wondered if anything ever shook that placid
look from his face. It was impossible to read his
real thoughts, but he must be enjoying himself, for
his partner positively sparkled.

Her musing was brought to a stop by her companion's rather stilted English. 'I leave you here,'
he said formally. 'Adam returns soon, I think. I
have to dance with others.' He waved an expres-
sive hand, taking in half the hall. 'You will sit here,
please.'

Perhaps Adam had arranged for her to be parked
in the alcove half hidden behind a great bank of
flowers and ferns. Christina said goodbye to her
partner, quite glad to see him go, for he danced
badly, and settled down to wait. There was still no
sign of Adam, but it would be easy to miss him
on the crowded floor. Several of the Ward Sisters

she knew danced past and waved, and she waved back, and presently Duert came into view, this time with a tall blonde girl. She didn't think he had seen her, and hoped he hadn't, although she was not sure why.

She sat through that dance and the next. Probably if she had gone on to the dance floor she would have found herself a partner, but she was shy of doing this—besides, Adam might come to look for her. She had a splendid view of the dancers although she wasn't easily seen herself, only by Duert ter Brandt who kept her under his eye without appearing to do so.

Christina was getting a little impatient and was on the point of making up her mind to leave her alcove when she was surprised to see Truus creeping along the wall towards her. She got up and went to meet her, putting an arm round her and sitting her down in the chair she had just left. 'Truus, you're ill,' she said urgently. 'What is it?'

'A pain—here.' Truus put a cautious hand on her stomach. 'And I feel so strange—I think I want to be sick.'

Christina looked round her. The dance floor was packed and no one was looking in their direction, nor was there anyone she knew in sight. There was a door behind her, if she could get Truus through it and back into the hospital itself... She turned back to her friend and was alarmed to see that her white face had taken a greenish tinge. 'Truus—' she began, and was gently interrupted by the doctor's deep voice.

'Something's wrong?' He bent over Truus for a moment. 'If you will open the door, Christina, I'll carry her back to the surgical floor.' He added as an afterthought, 'You might come with us.'

She hurried ahead, opening and shutting doors and then waiting at the open lift door. Truus was moaning softly and the doctor spoke to her in a comforting murmur. As the lift stopped he said: 'Straight into the side ward on the left, Chrissy— get the bed turned down and then fetch the nurse on duty.'

She was turning to obey him when Truus put out an urgent hand. 'Don't go,' she whispered, and caught Christina's dress in an urgent hand. The gathers were ripped, but Christina didn't notice, and when she did she tucked the torn flounces into her waistband and forgot about it.

'Now telephone Night Sister, my Registrar and the Directrice, in that order,' Dr ter Brandt ordered in his calm voice.

She did that too and went back to find that Truus was lying on the bed being examined. Presently the doctor straightened up. 'Appendix,' he said to no one in particular. 'I want her up in theatre in ten minutes.'

His eye fell upon Christina hovering at the open

door. 'You had better stay with her until she's an-
aesthetised,' he suggested, and turned away to
speak to the Directrice, who, despite the plum velvet, was already in command of the situation.
Someone brought a gown for Christina and she
bundled into it, and as soon as Truus was ready,
went with the trolley on the brief journey to the
theatre block. Night Theatre Sister was already
there, so was her nurse. Christina could see them
through the glass porthole in the anaesthetic room,
laying up a trolley. She smiled down at Truus, now
dozing under the influence of the drug the doctor
had given her, and when she opened a hazy eye,
squeezed her hand.

They took her away presently and Christina
started to take off her gown. She didn't feel like
going back to the dance, but she would have to in
case Adam was looking for her. She was halfway
to the door when one of the nurses came out with
a message from Dr ter Brandt. Would she be good
enough to wait in Sister's Office until he was
ready—about twenty minutes.

She sat quietly in the little room thinking of
nothing, feeling tired now. She looked up in surprise when Duert came in; the twenty minutes had
gone very quickly. He was still wearing his green
theatre gear and she realised with surprise that he
must have been operating.

'Is Truus OK?' she asked.

'Yes—I'll be ten minutes,' he told her, and opened the door wider to allow the Directrice to enter. Christina stood up, but was waved back into her chair, while her companion, once more in the plum velvet, went to the small mirror and examined her hair and face.

'You will say nothing, if you please, Zuster Forbes,' she remarked. 'It is not likely that we have been missed and Dr ter Brandt does not want the evening spoilt for his guests. No one saw you?'

'Only the doctor—everyone was dancing and Truus was against the wall and I was half hidden by some flowers.'

The Directrice nodded, satisfied. 'That is good. As soon as Truus is conscious we will return to the dancing.'

'Poor Truus,' said Christina, 'I hope she gets well quickly.'

The Directrice went away then and Christina sat on, not thinking about anything much. After ten minutes both the Doctor and the Directrice came back together. 'She's conscious—just,' said Dr ter Brandt. 'Will you take a look, I daresay she will want to see you.'

Christina went back to the side ward. Truus was nicely round and on the point of dropping off to sleep. She smiled a little at Christina and muttered: 'Thank you,' before she closed her eyes, and after a minute or two Christina said goodbye to the night nurse looking after her and went back into the corridor. There seemed little point in going back to the theatre block, and no one had suggested that she should. She began to walk slowly towards the swing doors which would lead her to the stairs and dance hall.

She hadn't reached the doors when Duert came through them. He looked so cool and elegant that she was hard put to it to remember that ten minutes earlier he had been wearing a green theatre shirt and trousers and wellington boots. He said at once in a brisk no-nonsense voice: 'I've asked the Directrice to go on ahead. We'll go in a few minutes, my Registrar will stay for a while to make sure Truus is all right.' His eyes surveyed her. 'You're a bit untidy, and your dress is torn.'

Christina was suddenly angry. 'Well, what do you expect?' she snapped. 'There wasn't much time to mend my dress or do my hair, was there?'

He put out a hand as she made to pass him, holding her with an arm round her shoulders. 'My poor girl—what a thoughtless fool I am! You shall have time to stitch your gown and do whatever you need to your hair—what is more, we will have coffee before we return.'

He swept her through the door, still with an arm round her, took a lift to the ground floor where he guided her through several narrow passages and opened a door into a large apartment, used apparently as a board meeting room. 'Sit down,' he invited her kindly, and pressed a bell, and when a porter came, ordered coffee and a work basket, and when the astonished man had gone, told her to go through the door at the other end of the room. 'There's a cloakroom there with a mirror and so on,' he said. 'Do you need a comb?'

Christina said no, thank you in a surprised voice and did as she was bid. The cloakroom was well lighted and it had a good mirror. She did her face, and because her hair was in danger of falling down, unpinned it and swept it into a knot low on her neck and went back to the doctor.

The coffee had arrived and smelled delicious. Her nose twitched with pleasure and Duert, looking at her from half closed lids, smiled faintly.

'You be mother,' he invited. 'They've brought sandwiches too, thank God; I'm famished.'

And so, thought Christina, am I. She drank her coffee and ate her share, then almost choked when he remarked casually: 'Your hair looks much nicer like that—you didn't look like you with all those loops and things.'

She gazed at him in astonishment. 'Like this?' she repeated. 'But I do it like this every day.' She went on: 'Adam says…' and then went pink.

'Ah, yes, of course. Well, don't let an out-of-date old fogey like me influence you.' He sounded serious, but she thought that he was secretly amused.

'I don't intend to, Dr ter Brandt.' She had pulled the sewing basket to her and was searching for a needle and thread. There was only one needle, a thick thing which would mark the delicate fabric of her dress. She sighed a little thinking of all the money she had spent and now it wouldn't be fit to be worn again. There was black cotton and white and nothing else; she chose the black and mended the gathers as best she could. It looked a botched-up job when she had done, but the doctor assured her that no one would notice, and she took comfort from his words. He got up to go when she had replaced her sewing things and she was conscious of regret. They had hardly spoken to each other, but she had found his company restful.

They slipped back into the hall through a small side door and Duert at once gathered her into his arms and danced her off into the centre of the floor, and since he was greeted by a number of people in a perfectly normal fashion it seemed likely that no one had missed him. They wouldn't have missed Christina; she didn't know many of the people there and she was hardly a conspicuous figure in the grey dress.

The dance went on for quite a long time and she began to enjoy herself. Duert danced very well, nothing startling, but he was nicely up-to-date with the newest steps. When the band stopped playing her took her arm. 'There's Adam,' he pointed out. 'I'm sure you must be anxious to get back to him.'

Adam was angry, she saw that at once, and she would have liked Duert to stay talking for a few minutes, but he merely thanked her politely for the dance and disappeared into the crowd of dancers.

'And where have you been?' asked Adam. There was a nasty edge to his voice.

'Oh, dancing,' she said quite truthfully, 'and I sat over there in that alcove for a bit. One of your friends told me to until you came back. Only you didn't.'

He frowned. 'Well, I got held up. And what have you done to your hair?' His eye fell on the mended dress. 'And your dress...you're not fit to be seen!'

It was a pity she had been told to say nothing about Truus, but even so Adam didn't need to be so bad-tempered. She said coolly: 'You mean to be seen with you, don't you, Adam?'

She turned on her heel and slipped through the dancing couples. Safely on the other side of the hall, she whisked through a door and started along the passage, intent on getting away. Her room, she fought fiercely, a pot of tea and her bed...

'And where are you off to?' asked Duert ter Brandt. He had come out of another door further along the passage and was waiting for her.

She stopped in front of him. 'My bed,' she told him in a quiet little voice.

'You're leaving Adam? It's barely midnight—we dance until the early hours, you know.'

She couldn't think of anything to say; just lately, she thought wearily, she had lost her cool composure completely. Not so long ago she would have dealt with such a situation with calm and dignity, but then until she had met Adam, she hadn't been in situations such as this one.

'He upset you?' The question was quietly put and she had nodded without thinking. 'Shall we go back and put it right?'

'No—no, thank you. You're very kind. It's all so silly...'

He smiled. 'Tomorrow you will see each other and laugh together about it.'

'Yes—you don't mind if I go to bed? I've enjoyed my evening...'

His eyebrows rose. 'Now that is a fib, Chrissy. Never mind, we must make it up to you one day. I'm very grateful for your help with Truus—you're a sensible girl too.'

It would have been so nice if he could have said beautiful instead of sensible. She smiled politely and wished him goodnight and went on her way. The stitches in her dress had given way again, and the torn flounce trailed forlornly behind her as she went.

CHAPTER SIX

CHRISTINA HAD TOLD Duert ter Brandt that she was tired, but in actual fact, once she was in bed she had never felt so wide awake. Perhaps, she thought uneasily, she shouldn't have left Adam like that; he had invited her to the ball in the first place and probably he had been delayed. Tomorrow she would beg his pardon and everything would be right again. And then there was her dress; she would have to get some matching thread and mend the tear properly. She wasn't very likely to go out again, but just supposing she did, she had no chance of buying a new one. She closed her eyes; tomorrow was a day like any other and she would need her sleep. She must remember to get flowers or something similar for Truus. She might go and see her before she went on duty in the morning—she could eat her breakfast quickly...

That meal was taken up almost entirely by excited talk about the ball and poor Truus. The news had already spread around the hospital, and Christina found herself the centre of interest and a good deal of sympathy.

'Such a splendid ball,' declared one of the Sis-

ters, 'and you had so distinguished a partner.'
There was a little silence and Leenie said quickly,
'I saw you dance with Dr ter Brandt—is he not
splendid?'

'Oh, yes,' said Christina composedly. 'He
looked very handsome. The dresses were beautiful—there was a white dress with sequins…'

The conversation took a lighter tone and lasted
until she rose from the table. 'To see Truus before
I go on duty,' she explained.

Truus was awake; she looked pale and tired but
declared that she felt fine. 'You were kind,' she
said gratefully. 'I think I would have fainted if you
had not seen me. Why were you not dancing?'

'Adam had to dance with some people he knew.'

Truus looked as if she was going to say something and then thought better of it. 'The work in
the Accident Room, who is to do it?' she wanted
to know.

'Someone called Nanda Staal.'

Truss sniffed. 'Her—she is *trots* and will not
work.'

'What's *trots*?' queried Christina.

'Proud—she does not like to make her hands
dirty or spoil her nails. She has many boy-friends.'

'Then you must come back as soon as you can,'
said Christina. 'Now, I must go or I'll be late and
Zuster Bunsma will be cross.'

'Oh, no, she will not—I heard her tell Dr ter Brandt that you were a good nurse.'

Christina had the urge to ask if the doctor had had anything to say to that, but instead she said cheerfully: 'How kind of her. I'll come and see you when I'm off duty—everyone's coming when they've got a minute.'

If she didn't hurry she was going to be late. She nipped along to the lifts; all three were miles away on other floors, and it would be quicker to take to the stairs. She was tearing down the first flight when she found herself stopped by Duert ter Brandt, very correctly dressed in sober grey, mounting the stairs in a leisurely fashion.

'Fire or haemorrhage, Sister?' he asked evenly.

She had stopped dead in her tracks for the simple reason that there was far too much of him to pass. She said breathlessly. 'I'm late, sir,' and since he was looking at her gravely with no sign of a smile: 'The lifts were engaged, I thought it would be quicker if I used the stairs. I'm sorry I was running.' She stopped, much struck by a thought. 'Aren't nurses allowed to run in Holland either?'

'I imagine nurses are not allowed to run in any hospital. You didn't sleep.' It wasn't a question, and she flushed.

'I expect I was over-excited.' It sounded a tame excuse and Duert looked down his handsome nose at her. 'After your hilarious evening? Two dances with my brother, a couple more with junior doctors and then hidden away behind the flowers...'

Her grey eyes flashed. She said icily: 'You forget, I danced with you—enough to turn any girl's head.' She added for good measure: 'I hate you!'

He stood aside and she rushed past him, going at a great rate, running at top speed, expecting to hear his voice reprimanding her. Instead she heard him laugh. She was almost at the Accident Room door when she paused, bewildered. She had behaved like a stupid idiot at utter variance to her usual calm. Dr ter Brandt had spoken the truth, but there had been neither mockery nor scorn in his voice; he had simply stated a fact in that calm voice of his—and she had been abominably rude. Her cheeks flamed remembering her schoolgirlish outburst. Of course she didn't hate him. She opened the door and went in, wondering if he would tell her that she wasn't suitable after all, and suggest in that pleasant voice which betrayed nothing that she should return to England.

She had to stop thinking about it then, because the Accident Room was teeming...old ladies who had fallen down and fractured a femur, small children with cut heads, bigger children who had fallen into one of the many canals in the city, elderly gentlemen with cardiac trouble...they were all there and seemingly in greater strength than usual. Christina set to work with a will. She had learned

most of the necessary words by now and her eyes
told her as much, sometimes more, than her ears.
Zuster Bunsma, after a brisk good morning, as-
signed her patients and marched away to deal with
a particularly nasty heart attack. Christina worked
on her own, barely noticing Nanda Staal, although
she did notice that she herself had far more patients
allotted to her than usual. She was glad of it, actually, for the morning passed quickly and midday
dinner was a snatched meal because Nanda was off
duty for the afternoon.

It became quieter as the day wore on and Christina had time to wonder if she should apologise to
Duert ter Brandt, but the question was when? She
wasn't off duty until five o'clock and she would
barely have time to change and go along to her
lesson. Perhaps tomorrow morning, she decided,
and realised that all day she had been expecting a
call to the office.

She had seen nothing of Adam, and in a way
she was glad, although she hoped they might meet
as she went off duty, but by the time she left the
Accident Room she was tired and so didn't much
care whether she saw him or not. Nanda had
proved as tiresome as Truus had warned; never
where she was wanted and far too careful not to
get involved in the messier cases. Christina aware
that her normal calm was ruffled, hurried to
shower, change, gather together her lesson books,

and start on her short walk to Mijnheer Beek's house. The entrance hall was full of people armed with plastic bags and flowers, waiting impatiently for the visiting hour to begin, and she wormed her way through them and reached the door. It was being held open for her and she darted through with a breathless '*Dank U wel*' to discover that it was Dr ter Brandt propping it open. The sight of him put her in mind of what she had to do; never mind if she was late for her lesson, here was the opportunity she hadn't hoped to have. She stopped on the top step.

Not waiting to plan her speech, she spoke quickly, wanting to get it off her chest. 'I meant to come to your office,' she told him earnestly, 'to apologise, you know, but we had rather a busy day and I have a lesson this evening and there wasn't time.'

'And what were you going to apologise for?' asked the doctor. He was leaning against one of the double doors which was impeding the passage of those going in and out, and she put out a hand and twitched his sleeve.

'You're in the way,' she said matter-of-factly, and then: 'I was abominably rude to you. I do beg your pardon, and if you think I'm saying it because I'm afraid you might give me the sack, I'm not.'

His mouth twitched faintly. 'No, I would never think that, Christina. So you don't hate me?' and when she shook her head, 'But you're not sure if you like me, either, are you?' He laughed, and she thought how very good-looking he was. 'Neither was your head turned, was it? Your so sensible head, it's already been turned by Adam, hasn't it?'

She stared up into his blue eyes and wished she could think of something dignified and crushing to say, only she couldn't. What she did say was: 'You don't like Adam and me being friends, do you?'

'No—at least, I have no objection to you being friends, Christina.' He sighed. 'You're on your way to Mijnheer Beek? I'll walk with you, I have to see him about a small matter.'

She stood her ground. 'There's no need,' she told him in her calm way, and he agreed with her readily; too readily for politeness, she considered, and then he added surprisingly:

'But I feel that no opportunity should be lost in getting to know each other.'

He started down the steps, and she, mindful of the fact that she was already late for her lesson, went with him. 'Why?' she asked.

They crossed the forecourt and started along the pavement outside.

'Because I feel sure that we shall have a good deal to do with each other in the future.'

She blushed which made her really rather pretty; he glanced sideways at her and then quickly away again. 'Oh—because of Adam and me…but you don't approve.'

He took her arm and crossed the street. 'My dear girl, does that matter? You're old enough and wise enough to know your own mind.'

She said quickly: 'But Adam isn't?'

Her companion grunted, which could have meant anything at all; he wasn't going to continue the conversation. Christina enquired after the woman whose baby had been born in the Accident Room and was told that she was doing well; so was the baby. 'And I've managed to fix up her return to England,' observed the doctor. 'In a week's time, when she's fit to travel.'

Christina made some noncommittal reply and was glad when they reached Mijnheer Beek's house, a narrow building, squeezed in between two larger ones. The ground floor was a baker's shop, and Christina sniffed appreciatively as they went in at the side door.

The inner door, leading to the upstairs rooms, was a solid affair with a glass spyhole and an old-fashioned bell which the doctor tugged with some vigour. The door, worked by mechanism from the floor above, opened at once and a testy voice boomed down the steep staircase:

'You are late—I shall wish to know why, Christina.'

The doctor propelled Christina up the stairs and

followed behind. 'My fault,' he shouted cheerfully, 'I delayed her: she is not in the least to blame.'

They emerged on the landing above, to find Mijnheer Beek waiting for them at his door. He said something in Dutch to the doctor and they laughed together before he said: 'We shall say no more about it, but there will be no English spoken, if you please.'

'Oh lord!' moaned Christina, and Mijnheer Beek gave a great rumble of laughter.

The doctor had made himself comfortable in one of the old-fashioned overstuffed armchairs. 'Coffee?' he asked mildly.

So they had coffee, brought by Mijnheer Beek's meek-looking wife, and Christina made stilted conversation with her teacher while the doctor listened. It vexed her rather that he should do this, but on the other hand it put her on her mettle. She considered she was doing rather well when Mijnheer Beek observed dryly: 'She is good, Duert, she learns fast and she has a large vocabulary, but she avoids her tenses—everything for her is in the present.'

Duert smiled. 'So I fear for myself, but later she will understand the future perfect—it has such possibilities.'

Christina muddled her way through saying that she found the past tense much harder, and he smiled again, a small secret smile as though he were enjoying a joke.

He walked back with her presently, and it wasn't until he had wished her a grave good evening as they reached the hospital that she remembered that he wanted to see Mijnheer Beek about something or other. She turned to look at his broad back disappearing round the side of the hospital and decided against going after him; she had the nasty feeling that he had forgotten all about her.

It was two days before she saw Adam. He was waiting for her as she came off duty after her dinner, catching her arm and drawing her into a narrow passage where no one could see them. 'Angel!' he exclaimed. 'I've the rest of the day free—how about you?'

Christina smiled widely at him, delighted that he was so glad to see her.

'I'm only off until five o'clock—Nanda has days off and Zuster Bunsma thought I'd better be on this evening—as many as possible of us because there's some sort of competition on at the Kursaal for teenagers and she thinks they may start a fight.'

Adam shrugged his shoulders. 'Trust that old crow to expect the worst!'

'She's not!' cried Christina. 'She's severe, but she's marvellous when we're busy—and I daresay she's right.'

He gave her a charming smile. 'Don't let's quar-

rel about it. We'll go down to Scheveningen and
have tea, I promise I'll bring you back in time.'

It was a day left over from summer. It was only
when they got out of the car and started along the
boulevard that they met the full force of a chilly
wind. But it was exhilarating walking arm in arm
along the hard sand, and Adam was at his most
amusing and in a high good humour. Christina
wanted very much to talk to him about the ball,
but his mood could change so quickly and she
wanted her lovely afternoon to go on for ever.

They turned back presently and had tea and
oversized cream cakes, then because she was getting a little worried as the time was getting short,
Adam drove her back to the hospital, sulking a
little because she couldn't spend her evening with
him. Determined to be sensible, Christina said
cheerfully: 'Well, there must be dozens of girls you
can spend the evening with,' and was a little
daunted at his instant: 'Oh, yes—and I did promise
a girl at the ball…'

He didn't say any more, which was infuriating.
Christina reminded herself that she had no special
claims upon him; if she had fallen in love with him
that was her business. She bade him a cheerful
goodbye and hurried away to get into her uniform.
She had a scramble to get on duty punctually, sliding in through the door just as Zuster Bunsma
came from her office. There was little to do for the

first hour or so, a few minor casualties dealt with
swiftly by the Casualty Officer and despatched
home to their own doctors. Christina filled in her
overtime concerning equipment and the contents of
the drug cupboard, and was just thinking of her
supper when the telephone rang. Zuster Bunsma,
going over instruments with the student nurse on
duty, lifted the receiver with the air of someone
who had expected it to ring anyway. She listened
in silence, murmured a reply and looked at Christina.

'I am right—the Directeur warns me that there
is a fight at the Kursaal and already the ambulances
are collecting those who are hurt.'

Christina whisked into action. They were always
ready, but it was possible to be readier than ready,
and if several patients came in together it helped
to have everything exactly so; forms laid out, a
good supply of instruments, dressing packs, gowns,
rubber aprons…she advanced to the doors as the
first ambulance drew up and the crew opened its
doors to haul out a stretcher. A girl, she couldn't
have been more than fourteen, her head roughly
bandaged. Zuster Bunsma cast an experienced eye
over her. 'You take her, Zuster Forbes; Dr Timmerman is on his way.'

Dr Timmerman was nice; quiet and rather shy
and capable. He arrived just as Christina had her
patient ready to be looked at. It was a scalp wound,

not severe although it had bled a good deal, he dealt with it swiftly, with Christina handing things and then clearing up quickly ready for the next patient. The girl, in the care of a policeman, was driven home to bed; Christina wondered about her, but the place was full of teenagers by now and there was no time to speculate about her patients, only clean their cuts and bandage and give injections and hold their heads while they were sick. She had been busy for an hour or more when she found Duert ter Brandt beside her. One of the housemen had just stitched a small cut on a boy's hand and she was putting on a dressing and giving him an anti-tetanus injection. Duert stood without speaking until she had finished, but when she would have begun to clear up he stopped her. 'Let someone else do that,' he said abruptly, 'I need you over here.'

The patient was a very small girl, brought in with the rest, although how she came to be there in the first place was a mystery. Her mother had been sent for, the doctor explained, luckily she had known her name and where she lived, and her injuries weren't severe. 'Get her on to your lap,' he instructed Christina. 'There's a small cut on her shoulder I must stitch, but she's a wriggler.'

The moppet was plump and pretty with a tear-stained face and round blue eyes. She climbed on to Christina's lap without demur and the doctor standing, prudently behind her, produced the local anaesthetic spray, warning her jokingly that it would be as cold as ice cream. The child made no objection, although she twisted round to see what the doctor was going to do next, which would never do. Christina held the small head close to her shoulder and began, rather desperately: 'Once upon a time there were three bears…'

The child was diverted, staring open-mouthed, drinking in every word even though she couldn't understand one of them, while the doctor, sewing daintily on the small shoulder murmured: 'Definitely one of my favourite stories. And here, if I mistake not, is Mum.'

He spoke quietly to the rather wild-eyed young woman who had been ushered into the cubicle, put on the dressing, wished the moppet the time of day, thanked Christina for her help and disappeared. Christina saw him later, bending over an unconscious boy, and when she had time to look around her again, there was no sign of him. It was disconcerting when Zuster Bunsma said dryly: 'Dr ter Brandt has gone—you were looking for him?'

'No, no, not particularly. I was just wondering…' Christina felt her cheeks grow warm; as though she cared where he had gone!

Zuster Bunsma added severely: 'He works too hard; he has no life of his own.'

'Well, he could have,' observed Christina reasonably. 'I mean, if he ever married and had a wife and children...'

She was unaccountably depressed when her companion said: 'And that, I think, will be soon.'

The last of the teenagers went and there was only the clearing up to be done. The night staff came on duty and Christina went thankfully to her supper. It had been a tiring evening, she reflected, but she had enjoyed it too, she reminded herself, and she had had a delightful afternoon with Adam. She had a day off on the following day too, perhaps they would go out again. He didn't know that, of course, but if he wanted to find out when she was off duty, there were ways of finding out. She dismissed the thought in case she might be disappointed.

Most of the other Sisters were at supper. Christina, eating cold meat and cheese on slices of bread and following them with more bread spread lavishly with jam, joined in the conversation as best she could. She used a mixture of English and Dutch words with no grammar to speak of, but helped out with a bit of arm waving and a good deal of laughing, managed very well. Several of them went to visit Truus after their meal. It was a week since the ball and her operation and she was up and about again, with the promise of a return to her own room the next day before a couple of weeks' holiday. It was almost ten o'clock by the time they left her and as they started off to the lift, Leenie said suddenly: 'I am not tired, I will go for a walk, just for half an hour. Who comes with me?'

Four or five voices agreed at once, and when Christina hesitated, Leenie cried: 'You too, Chrissy, you are free tomorrow and can sleep all you wish to in the morning.'

So they fetched their coats and went out into the late evening. The lovely day had been swallowed up into a cloudy evening and before the night was out it would rain. They turned towards the centre of the city, declaring that a good walk would do them all good and they could get a tram back. It wasn't a very great distance, as they knew all the short cuts and presently came out into the Plaats, the hub of the pedestrian shopping centre, with its cafés and enticing showcases of jewellery and scarves and handbags. They wandered from one to the other, taking care that Christina wasn't left out of their chatter, and then, after a cup of coffee at one of the small coffee shops, began their walk to the nearest tram halt. It was while they were waiting at it that Leenie clutched Christina's arm and exclaimed: 'There is the Directeur—there, in his car. The girl with him—is she not beautiful? They say that he may marry her, but I do not think so. She is not—how do you say?—sympathetic to his work.' She added wistfully: 'But she has most lovely clothes.'

Christina said hearteningly: 'You're pretty too, Leenie,' and allowed her eyes to wander to Dr ter Brandt's car, waiting at the lights. The girl was stunning, staring straight ahead of her, looking cross, and as for the doctor, he looked as placid as he always did—he also looked tired. The lights changed and he drove on and the girls clambered on to their tram. It was later, when she was back in her room, sitting on the bed brushing her hair, that Christina fell to thinking about the doctor. He couldn't be quite such a dull stick as Adam had made out. Dear Adam, laughing and teasing, making her feel beautiful. At least, for most of the time, she amended honestly, but perhaps he only criticised her because he wanted her to look her best. The thought sent her to the dressing table to stare at her reflection. There wasn't much comfort for her there, her eyes were all right and thank heaven her eyelashes were long and curling, but her nose was nondescript and her mouth too large. If I were a man, she thought, I'd not look at me twice. The only consolation was that she didn't look anything like her twenty-seven years; no frown marks, no turned-down mouth, no grey hairs, but only little laughter lines at the corners of her eyes. Her skin wasn't too bad either. She slapped on some night cream for good measure and got into bed. Tomorrow she was free to do as she liked, anything could happen. She went to sleep and dreamt of Adam.

He telephoned while she was still pottering around in her dressing gown. He had a half day and how about a drive to Amsterdam and a meal there? 'We'll get back here about six o'clock,' went on Adam, 'and go out to dinner and dance if we feel like it.'

Christina said yes in a breathless way and rushed to borrow the electric rollers. She had washed her hair only the day before, but she hadn't bothered to curl it, and now, even though she had the entire morning in which to get ready, she got down to the business of making the best of herself. It would have to be the grey suit, she hadn't anything else suitable, but what about the evening? The grey two-piece would have to do, she hadn't worn it yet and she wasn't sure if Adam would like it. It was plain and what her mother would have called neat; certainly not the height of fashion, or at least not what Adam would consider fashion, but it would hold its own in an unspectacular way.

She spent a leisurely morning doing her nails, her face, and then her hair. The rollers had done their work well, and her thick brown hair bounced nicely around her shoulders. She put on the suit and prayed fervently that it wouldn't rain.

They drove the fifty-odd kilometres to Amsterdam along the motorway, going very fast. Adam was in tearing spirits and although he had said nothing about her suit, he admired her hair. 'That's better,' he had observed with careless charm. 'You know, you'd be a pretty girl if only you spent a little more time on yourself.'

But time was something she didn't have much of in the usual way, and how could she go on duty with her hair hanging round her neck? Zuster Bunsma wouldn't like it. She said so and Adam laughed. 'Don't tell me that you worry what that old dragon says about you—she's as old-fashioned as Duert.'

'He's not old-fashioned,' declared Christina strongly, and instantly regretted it, because Adam looked sulky and muttered something under his breath, so that she made haste to ask him where they were going and how she was looking forward to the rest of the day together. It took a few minutes to coax him back to sunny spirits and after that she was careful to keep their talk to trivialities and to listen with the proper amount of interest to amusing accounts of his work on the medical side.

He knew Amsterdam well, which was a good thing, weaving his way through a number of narrow streets until they reached a canal where he found a place to park the car.

'We'll do the boat trip first,' he told her gaily, 'everyone does, you know. We'll sit at the back, so that you can listen to me and not the guide— I'm much more interesting!'

And so he was. Christina was shown the patri-

cian houses bordering the Singel, the narrowest
house in Amsterdam, the noble mansions on the
Keizers Gracht and the Heren Gracht, the narrow
waterways leading from one gracht to the next. She
was entranced, asking questions as fast as Adam
could answer them. She left the boat reluctantly,
and if truth were told, perfectly willing to repeat
the trip there and then, but Adam whisked her
along Damrak, pointed out the Royal Palace and
the war memorial in Dam Square and crossed into
the Kalverstraat, a narrow street full of shops, some
very fine, some surprisingly tatty. Not the best of
the shops, Adam pointed out; the boutiques were
in the PC Hooftstraat or the Leidestraat. They
walked to the end so that she could see the Munt-
toren and then Adam declared that he had had
enough of sightseeing and wanted his tea. Christina, her head turned in all directions so as to miss
nothing, would cheerfully have missed her tea in
exchange for a visit to a museum, but that was
something she could do on her own later. Adam
took her to a café on the Leidesplain where she
drank milkless tea from a glass and ate a cream
cake. She could have eaten two, as she had had no
lunch and only a cup of coffee and she was hungry,
but Adam was already talking about leaving the
city in good time.

He drove back to den Haag fast, talking little,
but when they reached the hospital he leaned

across her to open the car door and dropped a kiss on her cheek at the same time. 'I'll be here in an hour,' he told her. 'We're going to have a wonderful evening.'

All the while she was dressing, her hair in the electric rollers again, she was worrying as to whether Adam would like her dress. It had looked charming in the shop when she had bought it, but now she wasn't so sure. But there was nothing to do about it now; she draped an angora stole around her shoulders—one she had had for several years but still flattering in its softness—and went down to the entrance.

Adam was in the car waiting. He opened the door as she reached it and she saw that he was wearing a blue velvet suit and an open-necked ruffled shirt; her dress looked staid and dull beside it and just for a moment she felt hopeless and dowdy and out of her depth. But beyond telling her laughingly that she looked like a grey mouse, he said nothing, only asked her if she was hungry.

Her spirits lifted at once, and she assured him she was as he drove into the heart of the city, parked the car and ushered her into the Chalet Suisse.

It was a pleasant restaurant and very crowded; they had a leisurely meal and Christina, her doubts lulled by Adam's charm, began to enjoy herself. When he suggested that they might go somewhere and dance she agreed happily, and it wasn't until they were seated at a small table in a dimly lit night club that she realised where they were. The floor show was just ending and she hoped fervently that it wouldn't come on again, although Adam had enjoyed it, laughing at her and teasing her light-heartedly. 'What a good thing we met, Angel,' he told her, 'for you would have become a real old maid otherwise. You're only twenty-seven, you know, and it seems to me that you've missed a good deal of fun until I came along.'

She laughed with him and when he suggested that they should dance, got up at once. He was easily the best looking man in the room, she decided, and thanked heaven silently that at least she could dance, even if she fell short of his expectations in other directions.

It was one o'clock when they left and raining hard as they reached the street. Christina hesitated in the doorway; she had nothing with which to cover her hair and the rain would play havoc with it, but Adam took her arm and began to walk rapidly down the street. 'The car's not far,' he pointed out, 'it's not worth getting a taxi. What a splendid evening, darling, though you really must get yourself some pretty clothes.'

They reached the car soon enough, but not soon enough for Christina's hair; it hung damp and straight round her face, and the mohair wrap hadn't been improved by its wetting either. She slipped into the seat beside Adam and thanked heaven for the dim light; she must look frightful. She would get him to drive to the side door where it was almost dark...

But for some reason he didn't want to. He pulled up with a screeching of brakes and got out with her into the brightly lighted entrance. They were inside when he turned to look at her. 'Good God!' he exclaimed. 'You look...' He stopped himself as he caught her calm eye. 'Well, you must see for yourself your hair's ghastly—you really must go to a decent hairdresser—suppose we'd met any of my friends?'

She felt sick, but she wasn't going to let him see that. She said quietly: 'Thank you for my lovely evening, Adam, I did enjoy it. Goodnight.'

She went quickly before he could answer her, half running through the quiet passages. There was no one about, which was a good thing because she was crying just a little, too unhappy to know why, not wanting to think about it. The lift whined to a halt and its door opened as she reached it and Duert ter Brandt stepped out. His sharp eyes took in the tears at once and he said vaguely, not looking at her: 'Good evening, Chrissy, you've got yourself very wet.' He took the stole from her shoulders and gave it a vigorous shake. 'That's a pretty dress you're wearing. I hope you've had an enjoyable day.'

'Yes—no,' sniffed Christina, trying to sound normal and failing utterly. 'It rained and—my—my hair's gone straight.' She was aware that she was being ridiculous, but she couldn't stop herself.

'So it has,' the doctor sounded casually interested. 'Straight hair suits you, though.' He added gently: 'You had better make yourself a hot drink before you go to bed.' And when she sniffed again, he handed her a spotless handkerchief, wished her good-night and closed the lift doors.

He was a very comforting man, she thought as the lift soared upwards. And that was funny, for he was almost a stranger to her, and yet whenever they met he made her feel…she paused, at a loss for a word. Important? Attractive? as though she mattered…?

She slipped into her room and went to look at her ruined hair in the mirror. It was frightful. It struck her that she hadn't minded in the least that Duert should see her looking so awful, and yet she would have given anything to have been able to hide from Adam's eyes when they had reached the hospital. Surely it should have been the other way round?

CHAPTER SEVEN

IT WAS THE BEST part of a week before Christina spoke to Adam again. True, she had encountered him several times in the hospital, passing him with a serene nod in a corridor, or wishing him a calm good day on the several occasions when she accompanied a patient for admission to a medical ward. And indeed, there had been little opportunity of doing more than this; the whole hospital was busy and the weather had given up any pretence of a fine autumn, with nothing but rain and grey skies, offering no inducement to explore the surrounding countryside.

It was just such a morning, gloomy and wet, as Christina got ready to go out on her day off. She had decided to spend it at the Costume Museum, have lunch and then browse through the shops and explore the covered arcades, and in the evening she could catch up on her letter writing in the Sisters' sitting room, sitting cosily by the big stove, listening to the talk round her and doing her best to understand it. She tried not to think about Adam too much. Her common sense told her that she would never be able to change into the kind of girl he admired; either he must learn to love her as she was or she must let him go.

The museum was all she hoped for. She came out of its doors at midday into a downpour of rain and the first person she saw was Adam, standing just inside the porch, staring out into the street. She almost turned and went back inside, only he turned round and saw her and the teasing smile on his face drove all her sensible plans from her head.

'Hullo,' he said, and tucked an arm into hers. 'They told me this was where you'd be! Let's go and have lunch and decide what we'll do with our afternoon.'

She forgot her resolve to treat him with cool dignity, and exclaimed with delight: 'Oh, Adam, are you free for the rest of the day?'

'Lord no, only until six o'clock. Let's go to the Pier. There's a taxi rank just across the street.'

'Didn't you bring the car?'

He hesitated so briefly that she didn't notice. 'No—I left it in the hospital forecourt.' He tucked an arm into hers and walked her briskly to the taxi and threw an arm round her once they were in it. He kissed her too, lightly on a cheek, and told her that she looked pretty and where had she been hiding for the best part of a week?

'Me? Nowhere. I saw you several times, but there wasn't a chance to talk. We've been busy.'

'So have we. I shall be glad to move to the surgical side—I loathe medicine. The appointment's only for six months, thank heaven.' He started to talk about his plans and didn't stop until they arrived at the Pier at Scheveningen. Apparently he wasn't going to allude to their last meeting or apologise to her. Christina found herself making excuses for him as he took her inside, gave her a drink and discussed what they should eat. Adam was in high good humour, laying himself out to entertain her, and presently he began to talk about the holiday he was planning. 'We'll fly there, of course, there'll be half a dozen of us—we'll go just before Christmas and stay for a couple of weeks.'

'Will you be able to get leave from the hospital?'

'Certainly—and you must too, Chrissy.' He put a hand over hers and added wheedlingly: 'Darling Chrissy!'

It cost her a lot to refuse; her tongue longed to say yes, but she didn't hesitate. 'I simply can't. Truus is getting engaged at Christmas and will be on holiday, the part-time nurses are both married with children, and I can't go and leave Zuster Bunsma with two student nurses—it wouldn't be fair.'

He took his hand away and his smile held a sneer. 'Don't be such a prig, my dear. The Accident Room managed very well before you came; you're only a junior Sister and easily replaceable.'

She flushed a little. 'Yes, I know that, and I'm sorry if you think I'm a prig but I'm not going to change my mind—besides, I can't afford a holiday like that.'

Adam said carelessly: 'Don't let that bother you, if you come it will be all expenses paid.'

Christina shook her head, and he hunched a shoulder and stared out of the window at the wide expanse of sea and sky, a uniform grey and the rain still pelting down. After a minute she said: 'We quarrel a lot, don't we, Adam? Perhaps it would be better if we didn't see each other...'

She kept her voice steady by a great effort and met his look with a straight gaze, and then was totally disarmed by his low voiced: 'My darling Angel, don't ever say that again! You're the most wonderful girl I've ever met, surely you know that by now?' He smiled dazzlingly at her. 'A future without you is unthinkable.'

Good sense warned her not to listen, but good sense had no chance. She smiled uncertainly and was lost, not seeing the flicker of triumph in his eyes. He caught her hand again and squeezed it gently. 'Let's look at the shops,' he suggested, 'and never mind the rain.'

She couldn't have cared if it had snowed or blown a gale. She was entirely happy—well, perhaps not entirely; right at the back of her head there were doubts, so vague that she was almost unaware of them. She forgot them entirely presently, peering into the shop windows while Adam pointed out the kind of clothes she should wear and lingered before a jeweller's window, begging her to choose the largest diamond ring there...

They had tea later and took a taxi back to the centre of the city, where Christina elected to get out, saying that she was going to meet some of the Sisters and go to a cinema. It wasn't true, and she hated lying about such a trivial thing, but she wanted their lovely afternoon to end now, not in five minutes' time in the glare of the entrance lights in full view of anyone and everyone passing. She thanked Adam for her lunch as he kissed her goodbye, a rather absentminded salute, but then she excused him. His mind was probably on the evening's work ahead.

She walked briskly away, going up Noord Einde until she judged the taxi to be out of sight before turning and retracing her steps. She didn't hurry; the rain had stopped and the streets were filled with people on their way to the cinema, the theatre or a restaurant. She stopped to look in the shop windows and then had a cup of coffee in a snack bar before making her way to the hospital. She was crossing the forecourt when she saw Adam coming down the steps from the main door. He was wearing a dinner jacket under his coat and had an arm round the shoulders of one of the prettiest girls Christina had ever set eyes on.

She stood still watching them get into his car and drive away and then she walked on quietly, her mind an icy blank, to go to her room, take off her outdoor things and go down to supper with the other Sisters.

When one of them remarked that she looked pale, and did she feel all right, engendering an anxious little chorus that perhaps she had started a cold, she agreed in a wooden little voice.

'It is better that you go to bed early,' said Leenie sympathetically, 'for you eat nothing. I bring you hot coffee presently.'

Christina hardly slept, but she hadn't expected to. She sat up in bed in the dark, stripping away her dreams from hard facts. She had been behaving like a foolish schoolgirl, and she a grown, sensible young woman who should have known better, allowed herself to be flattered, imagining that Adam, handsome, carefree Adam, was in love with her. She recalled what he had said to her over lunch— that he couldn't face the future without her. She put her hands over her face, stony with misery, and began to cry.

She fell asleep as it was getting light, and when she woke, thanked heaven that she had another free day. She would go somewhere, anywhere, and walk and walk until she was too tired to think. It had stopped raining, but thick clouds were racing across a dull sky, chased by a brisk wind. Christina made herself some tea, got dressed, put on her raincoat and a headscarf, and went down to the entrance. It was almost one o'clock by now and there weren't many people about—it was too early for the visitors and those of the nurses who weren't at second dinner would be on the wards or off duty. She looked round her quickly; there was no one who knew her in sight. She nipped smartly across the expanse of marble flooring and actually had a hand on the swing door when a large well kept hand caught her gently by the wrist and turned her round. Duert ter Brandt hadn't said a word; now he studied her face, so carefully made up to mask puffy lids, white cheeks and a pinkened nose.

'Oh, dear, dear,' he observed slowly, and when she tried to free her arm: 'No, my dear, it won't help matters by running away. Have you had lunch?'

She was angry now. 'No—I don't want any. Will you kindly let me go?'

'No. Did you have any breakfast?' His voice was quiet, but it expected an answer.

'No.' She drew a deep breath. 'Will you please let me go? I'm only going out.'

'In that case, we'll go together, because I am going out too.'

His hand upon her arm prevented her from doing

anything else. She was walked across the forecourt to where his Rolls stood, popped into the front seat, had her seat belt fastened and driven away before she could frame a single rational sentence. She sat silent for a minute, fighting a strong wish to put her head on the enormous shoulder beside her and howl her eyes out. Presently she said in a wooden little voice: 'I have no idea why you're doing this or where we're going, but I want to get out of the car at once.'

'Tantamount to committing suicide,' observed her companion placidly. 'As to why I'm doing it, it is my business to enquire into obvious signs of unhappiness among the hospital staff, and where better than a quiet café over a cup of coffee?'

He was driving away from den Haag, along the motorway to Leiden, but at Wassenaar he turned off towards the sea and presently when the road narrowed with fields on the one side and the dunes on the other, he stopped at a small wayside café, ushered Christina into its dim interior and ordered coffee. She hadn't heard him order anything else, but the plump goodnatured woman behind the tiny bar brought *Kaas broodjes* too. The bread smelled delicious and the cheese and butter looked mouth-wateringly fresh. Christina gave a small, involuntary sniff and the doctor remarked: 'Drink your coffee and eat up like a good girl, an empty stomach plays havoc with the emotions.' He smiled at her so kindly that she caught her breath like a small child on the verge of tears so that he said quickly: 'Drink your coffee, Chrissy,' and this time his voice was one which would brook no refusal.

She drank the fragrant brew and then, under his eye, began on the *broodje*. He ordered more coffee for them both, sitting back easily on the small hard chair, making conversation about nothing at all. But presently when they had finished he paid the bill and with the air of a man with a job to do, stowed her back in the car and drove on.

'We're going the wrong way,' said Christina as they passed a signpost pointing the way to den Haag behind them.

'No—we're going somewhere where we can walk.'

He didn't say any more, but turned off once more, down a lane which led through the dunes to the sea. Presently they passed a house or two and then an occasional villa, set well back from the road in a well laid out garden and then, surprisingly close, a church spire above the dunes and a cluster of rooftops around it, and a moment later the road curved and they were in full sight.

The town was small, tucked in behind the sea dyke and between the dunes. It had a long narrow main street lined with typical seaside shops, small and old-fashioned, most of them closed now, since the season was over. Duert parked the car on the short promenade, ushered Christina out of the car and led her down a long flight of shallow wooden steps to the beach itself. It stretched, wide and white, on either side of them, as far as the eye could sea, a choppy sea worrying away at its edge. There was a wind blowing, quite strong and cold, but the doctor didn't seem to notice it. He turned Christina round to face him, buttoned her raincoat under her chin and then took her arm and started off along the beach. She went reluctantly, for she had no wish to walk into a fierce wind, nor did she wish for his company. To be left alone to cry in some quiet corner would have suited her mood very well.

Presently when she had got out of breath she began: 'I don't really want…I mean, I'd rather be alone—I know you're very kind…'

He didn't give her the chance to stop walking. 'At the moment you don't know what you want, Chrissy, so allow me to decide what's good for you until such time as your head is clear of what might have been and your cracked heart is mended—as indeed it will be. And I'm not being kind; patients who come to the Accident Room don't want to be met by a long face and puffy eyes—they feel like that themselves.'

'You don't know anything about it!' Her voice was quite savage because she was so unhappy.

'Oh, but I do. I was standing at my office win-

dow when you saw Adam leaving yesterday evening.' The doctor added with a curious intentness;
'And why should you be so sure that he doesn't
love you any more just because he was taking a
girl he has known for years out to dinner?' He
paused and stood looking out to sea, not looking
at her.

Christina smiled sadly. 'He told me he was going back on duty—he must have known.' She said,
suddenly fierce: 'You've known all the time,
haven't you, that he was only—only amusing himself. I must have made a nice change from that
lovely girl…a b-bit long in the t-tooth and as
p-plain as a pikestaff…'

'I have often wondered,' observed the doctor,
'exactly what a pikestaff was.'

'Why, it's the shaft of a pike, of course,' she
told him impatiently, and made an effort to snatch
her arm away, without any success. 'Oh, why can't
you just leave me alone?' she asked him in a high
voice which she strove to keep steady. 'I daresay
you think I'm a fool, you'll be telling me presently
that I should have had more sense, being taken in
by all that romantic nonsense, but of course how
could you possibly understand—you don't know
what it is to love someone!'

He gave her a quick look from under half shut
lids. 'I'm sorry you think that.' His voice was
abrupt. 'I won't say any more; you wouldn't be-

lieve a word of anything I said at the moment, would you?'

He turned her round and walked her back, silently now, the wind howling and bowling them along at a fine pace, and back on the promenade he ignored the car and crossed to one of the hotels that lined it and which was still open. It was warm inside but quite empty. They walked through the restaurant to a small tea room at the back and Duert let go Christina's arm at last and said: 'Go and tidy your hair,' he sounded kind and impersonal, 'and I'll order tea.'

She went obediently to comb the tangle of hair into something like smoothness and powder her still pink nose, and presently found herself in the deserted tea room again, drinking her tea while her companion embarked on a gentle conversation which required no answering, let alone much attention on her part. But the tea had revived her and the walk had tired her nicely. When he suggested that they should go she got up quite briskly and went with him to the car, already thinking of what she would say to him when they were back at the hospital. He had been kind, she supposed, in an impersonal way, but quite indifferent to her feelings, only intent on getting her back to normal as fast as possible so that she would be the same as usual when she went on duty in the morning. He was callous, and it would relieve her feelings to tell him him so.

In fact, she decided, as she settled in the seat beside him, she wouldn't wait until she returned to the hospital, she would tell him now, very politely, of course, and she would tell him too that he had no need to worry that she wouldn't carry out her duties in the proper manner and that there was no necessity for him to concern himself with her private affairs as she was well able to manage them. He started the car and they went back through the sleepy little town, past the shops and the church, along the narrow road leading back to the main road. It was almost dark by now. Christina stared ahead of her into the brilliant path made by the car's lights. Too brilliant; she closed her eyes against it and went to sleep. Presently her head lolled sideways on to the doctor's shoulder.

He glanced down at her pale sleeping face, slowed the car and slid on to a patch of grass between the trees at the side of the road, slipped an arm around her and pulled her gently against his shoulder, then settled back in his seat. It was quiet and dark, and after a little while, despite the car's comfort, chilly, but he made no movement, his face so calm that he might have been sleeping too.

It was more than an hour before Christina woke up. She yawned and opened her eyes and then closed them again, only to sit up a moment later

with them wide open. Before she could say anything Duert spoke quietly. 'You've been asleep.
You will have missed your supper at the hospital—
we'll go to my house and have a meal before I
take you back.

Unhappiness had flooded over her like a choking
mist. She cried impatiently: 'I'm not hungry—I'd
like to go back, I'm tired…'

'You'll be even more tired if you don't pull
yourself together,' he spoke without a trace of impatience. 'Where is your pride, Christina?'

She began furiously: 'What do you know…' and
then stopped. He was right, of course, hatefully so.
She had been completely out of character ever
since she had met Adam, carried along on a wave
of make-believe. She swallowed back her rage and
said in a toneless voice: 'It's very kind of you to
offer me a meal, the walk made me quite hungry.'
And then as he started the car: 'How dark it is,
autumn turns to winter so quickly, doesn't it?' She
didn't wait for his reply, but once embarked on the
weather, she kept up a steady flow of chat, deliv-
ered in an over-bright voice, determined to let him
see that she had plenty of pride still.

She didn't look at him at all, or she would have
seen a look on his face which would have stopped
her in mid-sentence, pride or no pride.

They were in Scheveningen by now, but instead
of taking the main road leading to the centre of

den Haag, he turned the car into a wide tree-lined Avenue, lined with massive houses, each in its own grounds. Halfway down it he turned the car once more into a similar avenue, but much quieter, with houses, even larger, standing well back from the road. Even in the light of the street lamps they looked impressive, and Christina, relieved at being able to stop talking, fell silent, looking around her.

Presently she asked: 'Do you live here?'

His, 'Yes,' was almost curt as he ran the car through an open gateway guarded by stone pillars with stone lions sitting on them, and up a smooth drive, to stop before a great porch, reached by steps and leading to a massive door.

This was opened as they got out of the car and Christina saw Corvinus standing there. The doctor spoke to him as they went up the steps, and he answered gravely and then wished her a polite good evening and closed the door.

Christina looked around her with interest. The hall was rectangular, with several doors on either side as well as one beside the curving staircase on one side, leading up to a gallery above. The walls were panelled in wood painted white and hung with pictures and portraits, and the floor was black and white marble, strewn with silk rugs. Duert threw off his car coat, then unbuttoned her raincoat and took it from her before ushering her through a double-arched doorway.

The room rather took her breath. It was large and lofty and furnished with grandeur, and yet it had a few homely touches which reassured her; there was a stack of newspapers cast down on a small table near the great open fireplace where a fire burned brightly, a squash racquet leaning against one of the velvet-covered armchairs, a large shaggy dog curled up before the flames and a cat, obviously of humble ancestry, sitting on a small chair, washing itself. It paused to look at them as they went in and the doctor said: 'Hullo, Gertrude,' and whistled to the dog, who leapt to his feet and came tearing to meet them. 'And this is Thomas, rather elderly and getting deaf. Sit here by the fire. Corvinus has gone to fetch Sally, his wife.'

Christina sat down, accepted the glass of sherry he offered her, and looked about her while the doctor sat down in a large wing chair opposite her with the dog's head on his knee. At last she asked: 'Do you live here all alone?'

'Well, not quite that—there are Corvinus and Sally, two maids and the gardener who lives in a cottage behind the house. If you mean am I unmarried, then yes, I am alone.'

She blushed, because of course that was what she had meant, although she wasn't really interested. The door opened and Corvinus came in, accompanied by a small round dumpling of a woman, with a still pretty face and a nice smile. The doctor got to his feet. 'This is Sally, Christina, she will take you upstairs to tidy up. Come down when you are ready.'

Christina got up too and shook Sally's hand and murmured something or other, then followed her out of the room and across the hall, up the lovely staircase to the gallery above. For something to say, she asked: 'What part of England do you come from, Sally?'

The little woman paused to look at her halfway, smiling broadly: 'Somerset, near Castle Cary—Middle Netherton, miss.'

Christina's wan face lighted up. 'Oh, how nice! I—my home was just outside Yeovil—Little Stanisford.'

Sally beamed. 'I know it well, miss. My sister and her husband went to live there when he retired a couple of months ago.' She shook her head. 'I never did—such a small place as the world is, to be sure!'

They had been walking along the gallery as she spoke and now she opened a door at the far end and ushered Christina into a large, airy room with tall windows overlooking the side of the house. The furniture was large, old and beautifully polished, and the hangings and bedspread were in a rose-patterned chintz which exactly suited the mahogany's gloss.

'What a charming room,' observed Christina, and went to look out of the window.

Sally opened a door, indicating the bathroom beyond. 'It's a nice house,' she stated in her soft country voice. 'Much too big for the doctor—that is until he marries and has a family. His brother—you'll have met him I daresay, miss—he lives in den Haag, likes the noise and bustle, I suppose. He comes here quite a bit, though.'

'I—I heard that he was a partner...?'

'And so he is, miss, but the consulting rooms are in den Haag and he doesn't do much at the practice at present because he's working at the hospital.'

'Oh, I see. I—I have met him.'

Sally shot her a shrewd glance. 'You look tired, miss, and here's me standing gossiping. You've not been ill, might I ask?'

'No, oh no—just tired.' Christina smiled brightly at Sally as she went away, leaving her to wander into the splendidly equipped bathroom and wash her face and then make it up carefully before doing her hair. She would have liked to stay longer in the room, it was restful there and the garden below was a delight to the eye with its stretches of green lawn and beds of chrysanthemums; it would be a picture in high summer. There were trees too and a high brick wall, so that there was nothing to be seen of any other house. She looked her fill and then went reluctantly, downstairs.

The doctor met her at the bottom of the staircase. 'I usually have my meals in the morning room at the back of the house,' he greeted her casually. 'The dining room is rather overpowering for one or two—my great-great-grandfather, who built the place, had twelve children and probably needed all the space he could get.'

He was leading the way to the back of the hall and opened a small door into a fair-sized room with doors leading on to a terrace. Its walls were panelled in wood, painted pale green and the rug on its polished wooden floor was silk Persian. The colours of the silk brocade curtains matched it exactly. The table in the centre of the room was oval with cabriole legs and the four chairs arranged around it were upholstered to match the curtains. Christina thought they might be early Georgian, but she wasn't sure. The table was laid with silver and glass with a bowl of late roses in its centre, and looking at it, she was struck with the thought that Duert must be a rich man—it was strange that she hadn't thought of that before, but then she hadn't thought of him, only of Adam.

The doctor, watching her, had a very shrewd idea of what she was thinking; he said with unwonted briskness: 'Sally is a splendid cook. I hope you will manage to eat something.'

Christina took her place at the table and assured him in a composed voice that she had no doubt that she would do justice to Sally's cooking, and during the delicious meal which followed, she kept up a steady flow of conversation about everything under the sun, repeating herself frequently. Her companion, making suitable replies in a placid voice, made no attempt to check her, only when they had finished their meal and had returned to the drawing-room for their coffee and she had fallen silent did he say: 'You don't have to try too hard with me, Chrissy.'

She gave him a smouldering glance. 'You told me to pull myself together—well, I have.'

'Indeed yes. And now you will go back to the hospital and go to bed and sleep, and in the morning, if and when you see Adam, you will ask him about this evening and probably discover that you have been breaking your heart for no reason at all.'

She put down her coffee cup on the little pie-crust table beside her. 'It's nice of you to say that, but you know it isn't true. I've been a fool, but that's no reason why I should go on being one.'

'All the same, I think you should give him the chance to explain.'

She gave him a suspicious look. 'You won't see him...tell him?'

He raised his eyebrows. 'My dear girl, why should I interfere? Did I not explain to you that my only interest was in bringing you to your senses so that your work won't suffer?'

Christina got to her feet. She wanted very much to say something scathing, something that would take that look of calm self-assurance from his face, but she couldn't think of anything at all. She said stiffly: 'Thank you for my supper—if I could have my coat?'

He jerked the old-fashioned bell pull on the wall and Corvinus came trotting in. When he had gone again the doctor said pleasantly: 'You will forgive me if I don't drive you back? I have an engagement very shortly. Corvinus will take you.'

He held her raincoat for her and put it on and tied the scarf viciously over her head. 'I can go by tram,' she told him coldly.

'Don't be tiresome,' said her host in a patient voice which made her grit her teeth. He ushered her into the hall where Corvinus was waiting. 'Goodnight, Christina.'

The drive to the hospital only took a few minutes, and Corvinus, engaging her in conversation, kept her mind occupied. There was no one to see her getting out of the Daimler as he drew up in the forecourt, and it wasn't until after she had gained her room that she realised that she might have had some explaining to do if they had. It struck her forcibly then that perhaps the doctor had sent Corvinus with her for the same reason.

She was getting ready for bed when Leenie tapped on her door to enquire after her cold and offer coffee. They were joined by several others and it was late when Christina finally got into her bed. She had been sure she wouldn't sleep, but she had reckoned without her long walk and the claret the doctor had discreetly plied her with that evening. Despite her wish to remain awake so that she might think about Adam, she felt her eyelids drooping. It was strange that instead of Adam she found herself remembering very clearly Sally saying, 'Much too big for the doctor—that is until he marries and has a family.' As she dropped off she had no idea why the thought of Duert ter Brandt marrying should make her feel sad.

CHAPTER EIGHT

CHRISTINA WAS coming out of Mijnheer Beek's little house after her lesson the following afternoon when she ran headlong into Adam. For a moment she imagined that he had come to find her and then when she saw the look of uneasy surprise on his face, she knew she was mistaken. She felt the colour leave her face, but she said in what she hoped was a normal voice: 'Oh, hullo, Adam.'

She had had the impression that he was going to rush past with some urgent excuse, but now his face relaxed into the familiar charming smile. 'Hullo, Angel,' his voice was warm and smooth and she had to steel herself to ignore it. 'Did you enjoy the film? I thought of you while I was slaving away in Medical.'

She eyed him gravely. 'Did you really, Adam?' She wanted him to confess—she would have forgiven him a lot if he had done so, but he didn't. He laughed and ran a finger down her cheek, making it a caress. 'You're on my mind day and night,' he told her.

It was a pity that they were standing in a busy street, because there were a lot of things she wanted to ask him, but she doubted if her temper would stand the strain and the last thing she wanted to do was make a scene. She said hurriedly: 'I can't stop—Mijnheer Beek kept me and I've only just time to get back on duty.'

Adam caught her hand. 'How about tonight?' he asked.

She took her hand back. 'Oh—is it my turn?' she asked coolly, and hurried away, choked with a mixture of feelings—misery because he'd lied to her, triumph at her parting shot and a distinct nervousness at the idea of meeting him again. Her elation didn't last long, the thought of the months ahead damped it down so effectively that by the time she reached the Theofilus nothing short of running away seemed to fill the bill. She was halfway across the entrance hall when the head porter stopped her. She was to go to the Directeur's Office at once please.

She glanced at the clock; it was barely ten minutes before she should be on duty in the Accident Room. She racked her brains for the right words and told him that haltingly, but he shook his head and repeated his message, so she went up the main staircase and along the corridor to the office and knocked on the door.

The doctor told her to come in—in Dutch—and she did so, to find him sitting behind his desk, piled high with a conglomeration of papers and books and forms. He swept them carelessly aside as she went in and got to his feet. He wished her a good evening with remote pleasantness and begged her to sit down, and before she could speak: 'Yes, I know you're on duty at six o'clock and you'll be late—I've told Zuster Bunsma not to expect you for the next twenty minutes or so.'

Christina sat and looked at him, behind his desk once more, and wondered why she had been sent for, but apparently he was in no hurry to tell her; he sat frowning down at the papers before him. Perhaps he was going to give her the sack and found it difficult. She said, to help him: 'You wanted to see me—I expect you would like me to go back to England...'

'Now why in heaven's name should you think that?' he asked in astonishment.

She said with a kind of despairing calm: 'Well, I behaved very badly yesterday, didn't I? And— and anyway, I think I'd like to go if that's possible, but I don't suppose it is—it would mean breaking my contract...' And when he didn't say anything, she went on: 'I met Adam just now—just bumped into him outside Mijnheer Beek's house. You were wrong, you know.' She turned her head and stared out of the window and the doctor stared at her.

'Did you give him a chance to explain?' he asked placidly.

'No.'

'I think you should. A storm in a teacup?' His voice was mild.

She turned to look at him. 'No.'

'Then perhaps this is the right moment for me to offer you a job outside the hospital.' He put up a large hand. 'No, don't start babbling, Christina, just listen.'

'I never babble!' she cried indignantly.

'Er—normally, no. Mijnheer Beek has cancer of the lung; he will be operated on in three days' time, here, in this hospital. He has asked that you should be his nurse.' The doctor permitted himself a faint smile. 'He is of the opinion that his chances of recovery will be much greater if he has some sound reason for staying alive, and feels that correcting your rather sketchy Dutch grammar—for of course you would be expected to speak Dutch at all times—and encouraging you in the art of conversation in our language, might furnish him with the required energy to recover. He will return to his own home after ten days and you would go with him. There is no reason why he shouldn't make a complete recovery; fortunately he will be able to carry on with his teaching after a period of rest. Will you do this, Christina?'

Her wide grey eyes were on his face. 'Will I go back to the Accident Room?'

'You will have several weeks in which to decide what you want to do. If at the end of that time you wish to return there, we shall be delighted to re-instate you, otherwise I am perfectly willing to re-lease you from your contract.' He smiled at her, a kind, understanding smile, and she felt strangely comforted by it.

She took a deep breath. 'Very well, I'll nurse Mijnheer Beek. When am I to start?'

'He will be admitted the day after tomorrow to a room in the private wing, he will go to theatre on the following day and you will accompany him there and after that to the ICU until such time as we decide that he is able to be returned to his own room. There will, of course, be a night nurse, who will take over from you at nine o'clock each eve-ning. You will be relieved each day for your off duty, but I should be obliged if you would post-pone your days off for the first week.' He stood up. 'I think that is all, Christina, unless there is anything else you would like to know?'

'No—no, thank you. I'll do my best for Mijn-heer Beek. I didn't know he was ill.'

'It would annoy him very much if anyone knew.' He opened the door for her, then half closed it again. 'Christina, would you like me to arrange a meeting between you and Adam? Should you not be quite sure? There might be some good reason why he went out...'

'Thank you, I wouldn't want that.' She added with some spirit: 'I'm surprised that you should say that, Dr ter Brandt. If I remember aright, you objected to Adam and me being friends.' She frowned. 'Why are you so persistent?'

'I have my own good reasons. But I'll not meddle. Goodnight, Christina.'

She had no opportunity to think about the interview. She changed and went to the Accident Room as quickly as she could, to find it busy, too busy for her to spare even a thought for her own affairs. Later, when they were quieter and waiting for the night staff to come on duty, Zuster Bunsma told her rather severely that she would be missed and that it was to be hoped that she would return when Mijnheer Beek was recovered.

Christina was surprised and touched, for Zuster Bunsma wasn't given to praising people; she murmured suitably, wished the lady goodnight and took herself off to her room. She had told no one of the Directeur's request, but all the same, she was met by several of her new friends, only too anxious to discuss it with her. Over innumerable cups of coffee they talked until late, so that she went at last to bed and at once to sleep.

Mijnheer Beek, presenting himself at the appointed time, showed a cross face to Christina when he was ushered into his room in the Private Wing, but it wasn't only cross, she saw at once that in the clear light of the clinical little room, it looked a nasty colour and drawn. Of course, she had always seen him in the dim light of his curtained study and had never suspected that he was ill. But she knew better than to sympathise with him; she answered his caustic remarks with polite and faulty Dutch, and suffered his testy comments with calm. It took some time to get him settled because he made a point of doing exactly the opposite to what was required of him, but at last he was ready, sitting up in bed and glaring at her.

She glanced at her watch. He was to be examined at noon, she had been told, and it wanted only a minute or so to that time. She tidied the room with all speed and was straightening the quilt, oblivious of her patient's irascible mutterings, when the door opened and Dr ter Brandt came in. He wished her good day, speaking in his own language, and then addressed himself to Mijnheer Beek. Christina didn't quite catch what he said, but it had the effect of improving the old gentleman's temper, so that presently he submitted quite cheerfully to a lengthy examination. He even addressed a few remarks to Christina, and when she answered him with tolerable correctness this time, observed to the doctor that she had, on the whole, done him credit.

They both looked at her then, but she refused to be discomposed by it, standing there by the bed; waiting patiently until Dr ter Brandt thought fit to continue his work. Which he did presently without answering, which for some reason, put her out.

The operation was a success, which considering Mijnheer Beek's determination to do exactly the opposite of what was asked of him, was surprising. By the time he was back in his own room, Christina was tired out, what with coaxing him to wear the garb suitable for a patient going to theatre, explaining a dozen times why he couldn't eat his breakfast the same as he usually did, trying to keep him quiet after he had had his pre-med, and then escorting him to theatre, where she watched Dr ter Brandt perform a neat piece of surgery before going with her patient to the Intensive Care Unit; the day was well advanced by the time he was back in his own bed and she longed for a breath of fresh air, but she had promised Mijnheer Beek that she would stay with him, so she did, dealing calmly with his tubes and bottles, making her observations with meticulous accuracy.

It was almost half past nine when she finally handed the now sleeping old man over to the night nurse. She would have her supper and go straight to bed, she decided, but halfway to the dining room she changed her mind. She needed exercise; she would go for a brisk walk—she could always make coffee when she got in. She didn't bother to change but put a raincoat over her uniform, bundled her hair into a scarf and then left the hospital.

She was walking briskly along the pavement outside the hospital forecourt making for the pedestrian crossing when Dr ter Brandt's voice made her
jump and let out a squeak of surprise.

'And where are you going at this hour, Christina?' he wanted to know.

She came to a halt at the crossing. The light was
red and she had perforce to stand still. 'For a walk,
sir. I need some exercise.'

The light turned green, so she said a hasty goodbye and crossed the street to find him still beside
her. 'You've not had your supper?'

'No.'

'Good, we'll eat somewhere. Where did you intend to walk to?'

She stood still, looking up at him. 'Just anywhere, and I don't want any supper, thank you.'
She added composedly: 'Don't let me keep you.'

He said coolly, taking her arm: 'You're not, but
doesn't it strike you as absurd that two solitary
people should eat alone when they could keep each
other company? We don't have to talk,' he told her
kindly. And when she didn't answer: 'We could
walk through the park—I wouldn't advise you to
do so alone at night, though. There's a café of sorts
on the other side.'

Christina was still wondering how to refuse politely when he marched her through an open gate
and set off along a path between rough grassland.

It was lighted, not very adequately, and it was difficult to see her surroundings by reason of the dark night around them. There was a blustery wind too, making conversation difficult. They had walked for several minutes when she ventured: 'I don't think we ought to…that is, you're the Directeur and it really doesn't do.' She paused and went on awkwardly, 'Do you take the other Sisters out?'

He said silkily: 'My dear girl, is this your idea of being taken out? I happened to meet you and what could be more natural than to drink a cup of coffee together?' He added deliberately: 'Of course, I know I'm a poor substitute for Adam.' He took no notice of her sudden gasp. 'Do not imagine that I have singled you out for special attention, I would enjoy equally well walking with Zuster Bunsma or Leenie, or even that redhaired girl who works in Out-patients.'

Christina checked the laughter bubbling up inside her. 'You have a very catholic taste,' she told him severely.

He grunted something and walked her briskly forward again and within a few minutes came out of the park within yards of a small café, very bright and clean and almost full. The menu was a simple one, but the soup was delicious, and invited to try an *uitsmijter*, Christina found it to be delicious too; two generous slices of beef on bread, topped with fried eggs and a salad on the side. She ate it all and drank two cups of coffee besides, comparing it silently with the dinner she had eaten in the splendour of her companion's house.

She had been taken aback to find that he lived in such comfort—perhaps luxury was the better word. She stole a look at him now; his suit was of impeccable cut, his shirt was silk and his tie, sombre-hued though it was, was silk too. It was borne in upon her suddenly that he was a handsome man, his mouth was firm and his chin even more so. Why hadn't she noticed that before? Perhaps because his habitual placid expression masked them.

He looked up and she looked away, pinkening because she had been staring. Just as though he had been reading her thoughts, he observed mildly: 'You've never really looked at me before, have you, Chrissy?'

She put down her coffee cup. Something in his voice made her answer truthfully. 'Not—not to see you. I mean, I've looked at you, but not...' She came to a stop and he nodded gently.

'I understand.' He added casually: 'Have you seen Adam?'

She said quite fiercely: 'No, and I don't want to.'

He nodded again and called for the bill. 'Shall we walk back the way we came?' he wanted to know. And on the way back he kept the conversation firmly in his own hands, wishing her a quiet goodnight as they reached the hospital.

She saw him the next day, of course, and on the succeeding days too: several times a day when he came to visit Mijnheer Beek, but beyond giving her instructions about his patient and listening gravely to her reports, he had nothing further to add. All the same, Christina found herself looking forward to his visits even though his manner towards her was impersonal. Perhaps, she decided, he felt he had done all he could to settle matters between her and Adam, although she wasn't at all sure whose side he was on. She remembered very clearly that he had told her he didn't like the friendship between her and Adam, and yet he had done his best to put his brother in a good light, even made excuses for him.

In a way it was a relief when Mijnheer Beek was pronounced fit enough to return to his home, and she with him. The transfer was accomplished not without difficulty. Mijnheer Beek, as usual, took exception to everything, snapping away at Christina in his beautiful Dutch and sneering at her efforts to answer him in the same language. It was pleasant at last to see him sitting in his chair in the dark little sitting room tut-tutting over the various items of news Mevrouw Beek was entertaining him with. It left Christina free to go to her severely furnished bedroom and unpack her things. A fortnight, Dr ter Brandt had said, just to make sure that her patient did nothing foolhardy and to allow his wife to impose the routine the doctor had suggested. She welcomed it; she had been hard put to it to avoid Adam in the hospital. Indeed, he had on several occasions waylaid her, producing a charm to send any girl's heart beating fast, but although she could hardly bear to do so she had resisted it. She supposed she should feel pleased about that; she felt nothing but a kind of emptiness.

Duert called each day, but never at the same time. Sometimes he stayed only long enough to take Christina's report and take a quick look at Mijnheer Beek, sometimes he would stay for an hour, drinking coffee and eating the light-as-air biscuits Mevrouw Beek fetched from the baker's shop below, and Mijnheer Beek made a point of keeping Christina there, so that he might demonstrate to the doctor what capital progress she was making.

It was during one such visit, about a week after Mijnheer Beek had returned home, that Christina, having helped her patient to undress and dress again after his examination, settled the old man in his chair once more and helped Mevrouw Beek fetch in the coffee, obediently sat down to drink her own, the signal for Mijnheer Beek to fire questions at her about this, that and the other thing, to be answered in correct Dutch.

'She'll soon be fluent,' he observed grudgingly, 'although her English accent is marked.'

The doctor stretched his legs before him. 'I like it,' he said. He looked across at Christina. 'Let's hope that it won't be a wasted accomplishment,' and seeing her puzzled look: 'When you return to England.'

She stared at him. His blue eyes met hers guilelessly and he was smiling faintly, but she didn't smile back. She didn't want to go back to England, she wanted to stay in Holland, here in den Haag, at the hospital, because if she didn't she would never see him again. It wasn't Adam, she thought confusedly, it was Duert all the time, only I didn't know. She became conscious that both men were looking at her intently and mumbled something, and the doctor said smoothly: 'But that, of course, won't be just yet.'

Christina collected the coffee cups and carried them away to the kitchen where Mevrouw Beek was getting their lunch, and stayed there until she heard the doctor's measured tread in the little hall. He put his head round the door to wish them goodbye, passed the time of day with Mevrouw Beek, told Christina to be sure and see that her patient confined his activities to what was allowed, and took his leave. Christina put down the drink she was preparing for Mijnheer Beek and slipped on to the landing. There was a small window facing the street at the head of the stairs, and she peered out. The Rolls was below and Duert was getting into it. It was annoying that he should look up, just as if he knew that she would be there, and wave.

It was time for Mijnheer Beek's pills. She handed them to him and when he spoke to her, answered him absentmindedly, and what was worse, in English, so that he choked over them and had to be patted on the back.

As soon as he had his breath he said snappily. 'Where are your wits, my girl? You must speak Dutch at all times. You behave like someone in love!'

Christina blushed. She wondered what Mijnheer Beek would say if she told him that she was; suddenly, unexpectedly and head over heels. And so unsuitably too. And what would anyone, and by anyone she of course meant Duert, think of a young woman who, having given up a good job so that she might be with the man she had fallen in love with, switched her affections to someone else and that after demonstrating in no uncertain manner that her heart had been broken?

She went through the rest of her day, outwardly as composed as usual, even addressing her patient in a meticulously correct Dutch which earned his grudging praise, but behind her calm face her head was like a pot on the boil. To go back to England and never see Duert again was unthinkable, but on the other hand she wouldn't know where to look when she met him again. She thanked heaven that on the following day she was free in the afternoon, and she had heard him tell Mijnheer Beek that he would probably come about three o'clock. She could be out; she would stay out until the last possible moment too; that would give her a day in which to sort herself out.

Mijnheer Beek took longer than usual to settle for his after-lunch nap the next day. Christina flew into a skirt and sweater and since it was raining again, her raincoat and headscarf. It was barely two o'clock, but she wasn't going to feel safe until she was well clear of the house. She poked her head round the living room door, bade Mevrouw Beek a hurried goodbye and started down the narrow stairs. She was halfway down when the street door opened and Duert came up them, two at a time. He came to an unnerving halt on the same step as she was, so that they were squashed together, her face within inches of his chest.

'Oh dear,' said Christina, and uttered the prosaic words with so much feeling that he flung an arm round her as well.

'It's raining,' he said, laughing down at her, 'and you're going out.'

She leaned back a little and looked at him and then quickly away again. 'Yes—yes, I don't mind...'

'You're early—you don't usually go until three o'clock.' He stared down at her, his eyebrows raised in question.

'No—I… That is…'

He watched the colour steal into her face and grinned suddenly. 'Running away again?' he asked softly, and kissed her suddenly. The next moment he had released her and gained the top of the stairs and opened the Beeks' door.

Christina nipped smartly down the stairs and out of the door, intent on getting as far as possible in the shortest possible time. She didn't stop to wonder why she was doing this, even though she wanted very much to linger by the Rolls drawn up to the pavement in the hope that Duert would return. She saw that the lights by the pedestrian crossing were green and once across the street she could go into the park. The lights changed to red as she reached them and she stood fuming with a dozen other people, watching the stream of traffic. It seemed an age before the lights changed again and she actually had set a foot on the street when she was neatly hooked back on to the pavement.

'Beek's asleep,' observed Duert cheerfully. 'We'll take the car somewhere we can walk.' And when Christina made a small rebellious noise: 'We can't possibly tramp the streets of den Haag for the rest of the afternoon.'

She was bustled into the car and driven away

while she was still forming and discarding polite refusals.

They hadn't gone any distance at all when she realised the road they were on. 'We came this way...' she began.

'That's right. It's pleasant by the sea even on a day like this,' Duert said mildly. 'What do you think of Mijnheer Beek, Christina?'

He kept the conversation on their patient, ignoring her small efforts to change the subject, until they were within sight of Noordwijk aan Zee, when he asked abruptly: 'You are feeling better, Chrissy, about Adam? You've seen him?'

'No, I haven't, and I feel quite all right, thank you.'

He glanced down at her with an expressionless face. 'Yes? Ah, here's the sea. We'll walk the other way this time, shall we?'

He parked the car just where he had parked it previously and they went down the steps in the pouring rain, to stand on the beach and look at the grey, tumbling sea. 'Nice,' observed Duert, and took her arm.

They walked a long way, not speaking because the wind was blowing in their faces, taking the words from their mouths. They went quite a distance before he turned her round and started back again, the wind this time bowling them along at a fine rate. By the time they reached the steps Christina's face was glowing and dripping with rain, her scarf plastered to her head, but she didn't care how she looked, they raced to the top and ran across the promenade and into the same hotel where they had been only a few days ago, only now everything was different. Just for a little while she was happy because she was with Duert, who didn't seem to notice if her hair was falling down or the rain had washed away her lipstick, who somehow, without saying a word, made her feel beautiful. Nonsense, of course, she told herself as she left him to do what she could to repair her hair and face. He seldom looked at her anyway. But he had kissed her, she reminded herself, so perhaps he liked her a little, perhaps he was sorry for her, trying to heal her hurt pride, and yet he had asked her if she had seen Adam...

She raked the comb through her still damp hair and went back to the tea-room, and when presently, Duert suggested that they should return to his house for dinner, she raised no objection. She had always been honest and she wanted to go. It never entered her head to refuse; probably he thought her a fickle creature, but that didn't really matter, in a little while she would have to go back to England because he had so plainly expected her to, and she would never see him again.

Belatedly she asked: 'What about Mijnheer

Beek? I'm supposed to be back by six o'clock, but
I forgot...'

'I told him I'd see you home this evening.' He
smiled at her gently. 'Shall we go?'

At his house, she was taken to the same room
as before and only then deplored the fact that she
was wearing such a sensible outfit, with no glam-
our to it at all. She busied herself with her hair and
achieved a tidy head and then turned her attention
to her face, making up with care although she was
sure that the doctor wouldn't notice. But he did. In
the drawing-room over drinks he remarked casually: 'I like your hair like that—you're not a girl
to wear curls and waves.'

She wasn't sure if that was a compliment or not
as she thanked him politely.

No one had shown surprise at her coming again
so soon. Corvinus had welcomed her with dignified
pleasure and Sally had taken her upstairs with
every sign of satisfaction—almost as though she
had been expected. The lovely old house and the
people in it had welcomed her. When Duert married, as one day he would, his bride would be a
lucky girl indeed. Christina, exchanging small talk
with her host, fiercely suppressed a longing to be
that girl.

They dined presently—watercress soup, lobster
thermidor and a light-as-air soufflé, and all the
while the doctor kept the conversation away from

any personal subject. Christina, relaxing under his calm, amusing nothings, drank the wine he poured for her so that the future, for the moment at least, receded and only the delightful present remained.

They were having coffee round the fire in the drawing-room when the door opened and Adam came in. Christina put her cup down very carefully into its saucer and looked at Duert. He didn't look in the least surprised and certainly not annoyed; he greeted his brother pleasantly and told him to draw up a chair and ring for another cup, then began a conversation into which Christina was drawn willynilly.

Adam stayed for an hour, charming and amusing as ever, and it seemed to her that Duert was encouraging him. She was stiff with rage when at length he got up to go and walked deliberately over to her chair, saying: 'Well, goodnight, Angel—we must make a date very soon.' She just managed to turn her head away in time so that his kiss fell on her cheek.

After he had gone she sat silent for a minute or so, looking down at her hands lying quietly in her lap. When she stole a look at Duert she found he was looking at her with a faint frown.

'Did you know that Adam was coming?' she asked him quietly.

'Oh, yes—I asked him to. Am I right in thinking that he doesn't matter very much any more?'

She said steadily: 'Yes, you're right.'

He nodded. 'Good. One must look not once, but twice, Christina. It isn't just good looks and charm and a gift to amuse—one only sees those the first time, it's the second look which counts.'

'You must think me an awful fool,' she muttered.

'We're all fools at some time or other, you less than most, I suspect, that's why you found it so hard.' He glanced at the grandfather clock, a magnificent thing of bronze and marquetry. 'You don't need to go back before ten o'clock, do you? Would you like to see round the house?'

She welcomed it, because to sit there and make cheerful conversation with him was going to be beyond her. She didn't see his smile as she jumped from her chair, eager to have her thoughts drowned in a conducted tour.

There was more than enough to engage her attention; lofty rooms with splendid plaster ceilings and high windows draped in brocades and velvets, furnished with beautiful pieces, the wood gleaming with age and polishing.

'Of course, I seldom use these rooms,' observed Duert, guiding her into a small, cosy apartment beyond a vast dining room, 'but being a bachelor I seldom entertain as much as I should. Come and look at these portraits...'

They went upstairs presently and along the gallery, while he opened doors on to an endless succession of bedrooms and then took her down a number of narrow passages to where the smaller rooms in the older part of the house were. It was more than an hour before they went back to the drawing-room again and Christina, seeing the time, said almost at once: 'Oh, that was splendid, it's the most beautiful house and so enormous, only I simply must go, Mevrouw Beek might be wondering...'

He made no effort to detain her. Her things were fetched and she was helped into them, bidden goodnight by the attentive Corvinus and led outside to the car. It was still raining, but she didn't notice. She hadn't felt so happy for years. It wouldn't last, of course, but she was going to make the most of it all the same. She thanked Duert quietly for her dinner when they reached Mijnheer Beek's door, and he said nothing at all, only bent to kiss her gently.

She went to bed in a glow of happiness, her thoughts so vague that she hardly heeded them, but there was one thing she was certain of. She loved Duert.

CHAPTER NINE

CHRISTINA DIDN'T SEE Duert the next day; he telephoned for a report on Mijnheer Beek, telling her in a businesslike way that he would be away for two days and if she was in any difficulty, to telephone his Registrar. He hung up briskly, leaving her feeling flat. She wasn't sure what she had expected to happen, but she hadn't thought of him going away.

There was no reason why he shouldn't, she agreed to herself as she attended to Mijnheer Beek's many wants. He had taken pity on her once more, that was all. The sudden thought that he didn't want to see her again was so sharp that she dropped the glass in her hand and spent the next few minutes picking up the splinters while Mijnheer Beek, in the prosiest of Dutch, told her off for being careless.

But moping wasn't going to help matters; it was a cold day after the rain and a good walk would help to bring her back to good sense. Life had become a mess for the moment, but she had only herself to thank. She sallied out into the street and began to walk, without realising it, towards the hospital.

She turned the last corner, and saw it, looming above everything else, at the end of the street and the sight of it was very comforting, for was that not where Duert worked? She stopped in her tracks, struck by the absolute necessity to go and look at his home; only to look, because that was where he had been born and had lived all his life, where he ate and slept and entertained his friends.

She got on the next tram and sat impatiently while it rattled its way from the centre of den Haag to its elegant outskirts. The sea was close now, she could smell it as she got off and walked through the quiet, tree-lined avenues until she reached Duert's house. It was clearly visible from the pavement now that the trees had shed their leaves and it looked larger. One would call it a mansion, she supposed, or a gentleman's residence. She strolled along, peering into the grounds, and when a gardener came round the corner of the house with a rake in his hand, she crossed the road and walked slowly back again still looking. Looking at its dignified front, one would never guess at the comfort and treasures within. She stopped, remembering for no reason at all the girl who had been sitting in the doctor's car; perhaps he had gone away with her, perhaps she was staying in the house. Christina had had no idea that jealousy could be so painful. She just stood there, wishing in a silly fashion that something lovely would happen; if Duert were to come out of his house and see her and invite her in; or come along in his car and stop right beside her and call her name...

Her ridiculous daydream became reality. A car stopped with a squeal of brakes right beside her and a voice said, 'Christina,' and then, mockingly: 'Angel!'

She blinked and looked into Adam's smiling face as he got out of the car. 'Inspecting the ground?' he asked, and laughed gently, 'like a good general before the battle.' And when she gave him a bewildered look:

'You don't have to give me that innocent touch, Angel,' his eyes narrowed. 'You're a plain girl, sweetheart, but no fool. Transferred your affections, haven't you? And why not? Duert's the head of the family and very, very rich, with the family house and all its treasures, and he's made a name for himself besides. He could buy you anything you ever wanted and keep you in luxury for the rest of your calculating little life. Clever, clever girl!' He put out a hand and caught her arm in a painful grip. 'Shall I let you dream on, Angel, or shall I warn you that Duert spends his life being kind to those less fortunate than himself? The odd avuncular kiss means less than nothing...'

Christina reddened and he laughed again. 'Don't tell me that you're so naïve that you supposed he was falling for you? A couple of kisses and the odd meal? You amused me when we met, you were so unlike any other girl I'd ever known, but you're no different.'

She felt sick and ready to explode with anger, but she managed to take a calming breath so that her voice came out quite steadily even if rather high. 'It doesn't matter what you think, Adam— none of it is true.'

He said lightly: 'Probably not, but who's to know? And if you succeed in capturing old Duert, and God knows he'll probably marry you out of sheer pity; even he might not know either, he might wonder...after all, you made a splendid show of being in love with me...but you'd never discover what he felt about it. He's never been one to show his feelings.'

He dropped her arm and flung his own round her shoulders. 'Imagine being with him for the rest of your days and never being quite sure if he believes you married him for his money.'

It was outrageous; it didn't even make sense. She wanted to go somewhere quiet and think about it, but Adam didn't give her the chance. He was standing facing the house now and his arm tightened as he looked over her shoulder to watch the Rolls coming round the side of the house. Duert was driving; he turned smoothly into the road and drove past them slowly, his face impassive as he saw them. The moment he was out of sight Adam took his arm from Christina's shoulders. 'Oh, well, I must be off—my half day, you know, and I'm taking a rather special girl out this evening.'

She hardly heard him, and she certainly didn't see him drive away. After a minute or two she retraced her steps to the nearest tram stop. A great deal of what Adam had said was sheer malice; all the same there was truth in it too. Right at the back of her mind the hope had been growing that Duert was beginning to like her, and that might have been the beginning of something more, but now she might even find herself wondering if she really loved Duert or whether it was his wealth. But it wasn't, she told herself fiercely. If he were penniless she would love him, but Adam had sown a tiny seed of doubt in her mind. He had made her feel cheap too. His words would pop into her head each time she saw Duert.

Tending her patient for the rest of the day she wasn't her usual calm self at all, mangling her Dutch so that Mijnheer Beek pulled her up on every sentence she uttered, listening to her strangely meek apologies with disbelieving snorts.

It was a good thing that Duert was still away the next day, it gave her time to pull herself together, which was a good thing, for when he paid his usual visit on the following morning his placid face had an icy inscrutability which froze her bones. And it was made worse because she had no idea why—not that he kept her in suspense for long. He examined Mijnheer Beek, declared him to be fit enough to do without a nurse, suggested most strongly that he and his wife should take a short holiday and then present himself for a further check-up, refused the coffee offered him and invited her coldly to step into the dark little sitting-room with him.

'You will report for duty—er—let me see, tomorrow afternoon at three o'clock. Zuster Bunsma will be informed.'

It was obvious to her that he had no intention of saying more. She asked bleakly: 'What have I done?' and since the occasion seemed to demand it, added: 'Sir.'

'Oh, you have done well with Mijnheer Beek; it is a pity that your common sense doesn't extend to your private life. I had rather formed the opinion that you had had a change of heart about Adam.'

'Well, I have,' declared Christina, very much on edge, so that her voice came out too loud.

'Indeed?' he sounded almost lazy. 'And yet I saw you yesterday afternoon, in front of my house, of all places, standing with Adam's arm round you.'

Christina went very red, then white, so that her ordinary face looked plain and pinched. 'Oh, no!' she whispered.

'Oh, yes, Christina.' He gave her a small mocking smile. 'You should be more careful where you meet.'

'But I didn't—I wasn't—I only went there because...'

'You hoped Adam might be at the house?'

She shook her head. 'I didn't know he lived there.'

Duert said pleasantly: 'He doesn't. I'm surprised that you didn't know that, but he must have told you that this is the one afternoon in the week when he helps with the practice.' He gave her a long look.

'Why were you there if it wasn't to meet Adam?'

She stared back, wondering what he would say if she told him that she had gone there just to look at the house, because he lived there and it made him seem nearer. Not now, though. He had never seemed so far away. She clamped her mouth shut; there could be nothing worse than telling him.

When she didn't speak he said with the calm coldness which was much worse than an angry shout: 'You will be good enough to be more discreet with your personal affairs, Christina, although you are to be forgiven, I suppose, because you won't be seeing him for a long time.' His voice became expressionless. 'Unless he intends to take you to New York with him?'

Her mouth had gone very dry; it was quite difficult to speak. 'No,' she said finally.

He opened the door. 'Tomorrow afternoon, then, and I trust that when he goes you will have your feelings under control.' He was gone, which was as well. If he had stayed a moment longer she would have picked up the first thing handy, and flung it at his head.

It was quite difficult to carry on as usual, but she managed it. Mijnheer Beek, rather to her surprise, expressed regret at her going, although he was quick to point out that just as soon as he returned from his holiday he would expect her to resume her lessons and, what was more, study hard while he was away. Christina, a dozen plans milling around inside her head, assured him, with no truth at all, that she would and went to pack up her things, joined presently by Mevrouw Beek, quite tearful at parting with her. 'For you've been like a daughter to me,' she declared, 'and you aren't afraid of my husband, either.' She added: 'And your Dutch is now so good. You will stay in Holland?'

Christina wedged a pair of shoes into her case and slammed the lid. 'It's delightful here,' she said evasively, 'and Mijnheer Beek has been such a splendid teacher, I feel quite at home in Holland now.'

Zuster Bunsma received her back with a brusque

warning that two of the nurses were off sick and
they were short-staffed. 'And you do not look very
well yourself,' she remarked tartly.

'I'm very well, Zuster Bunsma, and I'm glad to
be back. Shall I take Zuster Smit with me and see
to that young woman with the compound fracture?'

Zuster Bunsma nodded. 'Yes. They have just
telephoned to say that there is a car accident on
the motorway, and we must expect casualties.'

It was good to be back, thought Christina, gently
easing denim slacks off her patient. She had had
to slit the seam to expose the injured leg and then
cut off the striped woollen sock. It was a nasty
fracture and the student nurse, who had only just
started her training, winced at the sight of it so that
once the Casualty Officer had arrived Christina
sent her to her tea; the girl would need it if there
was a bad crash coming in.

The first of the victims arrived ten minutes
later—an elderly woman with head injuries, her
hair full of fine splinters of glass, and hard on her
heels came an old man, his cuts and bruises not
nearly as bad as his state of shock. Christina set
Zuster Smit, back from her tea, to make him comfortable, take his temperature and BP, and search
gently for injuries, while she turned her attention
to the glass splinters.

Three more people arrived in quick succession.
Zuster Bunsma sent the second nurse to relieve her

and waved her urgently towards the Casualty Officer, already bending over the first of them. A young woman this time, pale and unconscious. Blood was coming slowly through the front of her sweater and Christina whipped out her scissors and began to cut the garment loose, to expose a round jagged wound.

'The driver?' she asked, and nodded at the bruises already changing from redness to purple. 'Shall I get this skirt off—I'll have to cut it.'

She bent to her task, vaguely knowing that Zuster Bunsma was busy close by and that there were several housemen there now. She was hardly aware of Duert taking the place of the Casualty Officer, she was fully occupied doing her own work, handing things to him without looking up. It wasn't until she heard his quiet voice say in English: 'I want this girl in ICU, at once, the left lung is perforated and heaven knows what else besides,' that she realised he was there.

She organised the porters and trolley and then, obedient to the doctor's calm order, accompanied the girl to ICU. She stayed to help for a short time and when she got back to the Accident Room, the doctor was with Zuster Bunsma examining the last of the patients, another elderly woman. Christina began to clear up. The two younger Zusters were already busy. Even with the three of them working flat out, they were barely finished by the time the

woman was warded. Christina was checking the
apparatus beside each couch as Duert went away.
He wished her a courteous good evening and added
his thanks as he went past her.

She went to bed late that evening. The other
Sisters wanted to hear about her stay at Mijnheer
Beek's house and Leenie was back on to light duties. One of the girls had got engaged while Christina was away, so that there was a good deal of
laughing and teasing. She joined in the chatter,
glad to do so because she didn't have to think.

But in her room later, in bed and very wide
awake, she let her thoughts roam. She wouldn't be
able to stay. Duert despised her, and to encounter
that polite, cool gaze each time they met was more
than she could endure. He had told her that if she
wished to break her contract he would allow her
to do so, and that was what she must do. Go back
to England and start again, she supposed, but not
London. She wouldn't be able to bear Hilary's
thinly veiled dislike or George Henry's worried
questioning. She would go back to her home; perhaps there would be a place for her in Yeovil Hospital. She thought with sudden longing of her
home. Life had been uncomplicated then and
surely could be again.

But having made up her mind, it was another
thing to carry out her decision. Duert proved sin-
gularly elusive, and it was another three days be-

fore she could get an appointment with him in his office, and when she finally got there, already slightly off balance by reason of a hectic morning's work and Zuster Bunsma's nasty mood, she found it almost impossible to take the chair he so coldly offered and repeat the calm and collected speech she had rehearsed far too often over the last few days. It came out in a hotchpotch of half-finished sentences and far too many reasons as to why she wished to terminate her contract. She floundered on for quite a few minutes while Duert sat back in his chair, watching her, his face inscrutable, his eyes gleaming with amusement. Presently he took pity on her.

'You need not make such heavy weather of it, Christina,' he pointed out placidly. 'I told you some time ago that you were free to go if you should wish.' He turned over the papers on his desk. 'As a matter of fact, I have an application from a nurse who trained here, for a post in the Accident Room. She is anxious to start work as soon as possible if there should be a vacancy.'

Christina felt as though he had, ever so politely, poured a bucket of cold water over her. She said stiffly: 'Then I wouldn't be upsetting anyone if I go quite soon.'

'As to that, I have no doubt that you are upsetting quite a number of people. You have made a good many friends while you have been with us.'

He half closed his eyes. 'But none of us is indispensable, or so we are told.'

'No—well, will you please tell me when I can go?' She felt empty. She had expected him to be angry, argue with her, point out what a mess she had made of things, and here he was telling her in the pleasantest manner imaginable that she could go.

'And what is quite soon?' enquired Duert conversationally. 'Today? Tomorrow? Next week?' He sat looking at her thoughtfully. 'It would suit me very well if you were to leave in a week's time—a Tuesday. What do you intend to do?'

'Go home. I can get a job at the local hospital— I worked there before.'

'Ah yes. Well, Christina, I'll arrange for your salary and so on to be given you when you leave.' He added casually; 'Adam leaves for New York on the same day.' He glanced up at her under his lids.

Christina looked back at him and didn't say a word. It wouldn't matter what she said, he wasn't likely to believe her. She got to her feet and said: 'Very well, sir,' and went out of the room. Probably he had had a mind to say more, but she wasn't going to wait to hear it.

She hardly saw him during the next week, and as each day flew by she longed for it back again so that she might have a chance of meeting him.

She packed her case, bore unhappily the surprised protests of her friends and still more unhappily Zuster Bunsma's pithy remarks about young women who should know better than to give up a good job where they were appreciated. 'And what is more,' continued that lady, 'you have taken the trouble to learn our language—you are by no means fluent and your grammar leaves much to be desired, but in time you would have done very well. A great waste.'

She had arranged to leave after breakfast, and although it had been taken for granted that she was returning to England she had done nothing about booking a flight. She said goodbye to everyone, ordered a taxi to take her to the station and then, although she hadn't intended to do it, went along to the Directeur's Office. There was something she had to say to him. It was unlikely that he would believe her, but since they wouldn't see each other again that wouldn't matter much; at least she would have got it off her chest.

It was fortunate that his secretary offered the information that he was free. Christina marched in in her sensible raincoat, a woolly cap pulled well down against the chill outside, her face white with the effort to remain matter-of-fact.

Duert got to his feet. 'Good morning, Christina. You are about to leave? I am sorry to see you go, but I hope that in a little while we shall meet again.'

'No,' said Christina quite violently, forgetting to be matter-of-fact, 'I don't want to see you again ever. You don't believe a word I say and you're glad to be rid of me, aren't you? You couldn't send me away fast enough. I just wonder what would have happened if I hadn't asked to go. And I'll tell you something—I thought I loved Adam, but that was because I—haven't met many men who took any notice of me, but it wasn't love at all—I don't care if he goes to Timbuctoo. But he liked to think that I was still in love with him.' She moved a little nearer to the door, ready to bolt. 'And I wasn't meeting him outside your house—he saw me there, and I'll tell you why I was there. I wanted to look at it again, just because you live in it—it's your home—I wanted to remember it...' She opened the door. 'That's funny, isn't it?'

She banged the door shut and flew along the passage and down the stairs and out to the taxi. When she got to the station she left her case at the luggage office and with her tote bag slung over her shoulder, went to find the bus station.

There was a bus on the point of leaving. She got into it, thankful to get inside away from the cold raw wind, and sat looking out at the passing traffic, not seeing any of it, certainly not noticing Sally, waiting to cross the road, staring at her in surprise.

The bus seemed to take an endless time, stopping frequently, its passengers in no haste to get off or on. After the Rolls it was unbearable, but it stopped finally and Christina got out at the end of the narrow street and started to walk down it towards the sea. Halfway down there was a café open, and she went inside and drank a cup of coffee before going on again through the almost deserted little town. The boulevard was deserted too, not to be wondered at on such a bleak morning. The wind was boisterous and cold, stirring the grey sea into angry waves. Christina shivered as she went down the steps to the beach; her raincoat was too thin and she thanked heaven that she had her woolly cap and gloves. She was totally mad, she told herself, a sentimental idiot, making a useless pilgrimage just because she had walked here with Duert.

If it hadn't been for the urgent buzz of his intercom, Duert would have caught Christina up easily enough before she left the hospital. As it was he was immediately involved in matters which held his attention for the next half hour, by which time he rightly judged that she would be gone—a fact verified by the head porter. He sat down at his desk again and sighed. How like Chrissy to make a statement to alter a man's whole life and then disappear. He rang his secretary, told her to book him a seat on the afternoon flight to Heathrow, trod through the hospital to the Directrice's Office, where he spent some time, leaving that lady in something of a flutter, had a brief discussion with the deputy Directeur and then returned to his own office to map out the shortest route to Christina's home. He had warned his colleagues that he might be away for at least four days, but he had to bear in mind the fact that Chrissy might not have gone to her home after all. Presently he got up from his desk, left instructions with his secretary and went out to his car.

Corvinus took the news of the doctor's sudden departure with his usual goodnatured calm, merely enquiring if he would be away for any length of time. The doctor paused on his way to his study. 'I have no idea—it rather depends on how long it takes me to find Miss Forbes.'

Corvinus hid a grin of pleasure. 'Yes, indeed, doctor. Lunch is ready when you want it.'

'Lunch?' asked his employer vaguely. 'Oh, I suppose so.' He went inside and shut the door, and Corvinus, walking fast for such a comfortably stout man, hotfooted it to the kitchen. Sally was straining soup with meticulous care, but she stopped doing it when Corvinus told her the news.

'But I saw Miss Christina this very morning—not two hours ago, on the bus going to Noordwijk. She didn't see me—she was looking out, but I doubt if she was noticing anything. Very unhappy she looked.'

Corvinus picked up the tray and went along to the small dining room, where he set the plate of soup before the doctor. He watched him sample it before observing thoughtfully: 'You'll excuse me, doctor, but you said you were going to England to fetch Miss Forbes back,' and when Duert growled an assent: 'Maybe Sally made a mistake, but she's sure that she saw Miss Christina on the bus going to Noordwijk, not two hours ago.'

The doctor put down his spoon. He had gone a little white, but he said in a steady voice: 'Ask Sally to come here for a minute, would you, Corvinus?' And when she came, a little breathless and excited at being caught up in what she privately believed to be romance with a big R: 'Are you quite sure, Sally? It's important...'

'Certain sure, doctor. She was wearing a green woolly cap and I thought as how it didn't suit her.'

'You're quite right, it doesn't. Did she look... how did she look, Sally?'

'White and worn down. She was looking out of the window, but she wasn't seeing anything, if you know what I mean, doctor.'

He smiled at her. 'I'm sorry, Sally, I'm not going to eat my lunch, I haven't the time, but you can make up for it by cooking something really delicious for our dinner this evening.'

'You'll want your car coat?' said Corvinus. 'I'll fetch it. Is there anything you wish us to do, doctor?'

Duert was already in the hall, getting into the jacket his devoted servant was holding out. 'No, I think not—yes, there is. Make sure that the guest room Miss Christina used is ready for her.' He grinned at Corvinus. 'And thanks to both of you!'

Christina walked northwards into the teeth of the wind, glad of the exercise, although after half an hour or so her steps slowed, because it was hard going. She turned round once to stand and stare at the little town, already some way away, dwarfed by the sea and the sky, turning from a uniform grey to an ominous black. Presently it would rain, but she had no thought of turning back, not yet at any rate. The blustery wind made thinking impossible and she didn't want to think for a bit. Already horror at what she had said to Duert was creeping through her head; even with no one in sight for miles around, she got red in the face just remembering. She tramped on, a lonely figure in a lonely landscape.

The first time she heard a whistle she didn't bother with it. It was so faint above the sound of the wind, it could be a seabird or even the wind itself. But when it persisted she stopped and looked around her. It wasn't until she had turned right round to look behind her that she saw Duert, com-

ing towards her at twice her speed. She dismissed
the instant idea that she would run; there was nowhere to run to and he would overtake her. She
stood still, wondering how on earth he had known
she would be there and what he would say.

He fetched up in front of her, breathing easily,
as though he were in the habit of walking miles in
a half gale. 'Are we going to the North Pole?' he
asked pleasantly. 'Or are you by any chance running away, my darling?'

She opened her mouth to speak and then closed
it again. Presently she mumbled: 'How did you
know I was here?'

'I didn't. Sally saw you in a bus, which was
fortunate, because I had arranged to fly to England
this afternoon and fetch you back.' He came a little
closer and put his arms round her. 'If you had
waited just one minute—but no, you go rushing
off, telling yourself that you're unloved and un-
wanted.'

Two tears trickled down her cold cheeks. 'But I
am,' she wailed. 'You sat there like an iceberg, t-
telling me that it suited you if I left as soon as
possible...'

'Well, I could hardly marry you while you were
still working at the hospital, could I?'

She glared up at him. 'Don't you say things like
that to me!'

'It slipped out,' declared Duert meekly. 'I'll start

again.' He held her a little more closely and pushed the unbecoming cap back from her face. 'I fell in love with you the very first time we met, only I thought that you and Adam...so even when you quarrelled with him, I had to encourage you to make it up, didn't I? I wanted very much to tell you that although he's my brother he's not quite ready to settle down yet—that he falls in and out of love just for the fun of it. I thought at first he was serious about you and then I wasn't sure, and when we came here that first time I longed to tell you, but you wouldn't have listened, would you, my little love? And then when I saw you both—I did my best to hold you at arm's length, for it seemed to me that if you went back to England and Adam was in America, then I stood a chance later on.' He lifted her chin so that he could look into her face. 'Do I stand a chance, my love?'

Christina smiled shakily. 'Oh, yes, I think I love you more than anyone else in the world. I don't know what I'd do if you didn't love me too.'

'That question won't arise.' He kissed her hard and then again slowly. 'We're going back home,' he said softly, 'our home now. We'll be married just as soon as the law allows and I shall buy you a new hat, because I can't like this one.' He turned her round and began to walk back towards the town, but presently he stopped and wrapped her tightly in his arms again and kissed her until she was breathless.

Christina kissed him back. 'We ought to hurry,' she told him. 'It's going to rain.'

'There are some things which cannot be hurried,' said Duert, and bent to kiss her again, just to prove it.

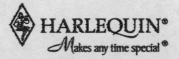

HARLEQUIN®
INTRIGUE

WE'LL LEAVE YOU BREATHLESS!

If you've been looking for thrilling tales of
contemporary passion and sensuous love stories
with taut, edge-of-the-seat suspense—then
you'll love Harlequin Intrigue!

Every month, you'll meet four new heroes
who are guaranteed to make your spine tingle
and your pulse pound. With them you'll enter
into the exciting world of Harlequin Intrigue—
where your life is on the line
and so is your heart!

THAT'S INTRIGUE—
ROMANTIC SUSPENSE
AT ITS BEST!

HARLEQUIN®
Makes any time special ®

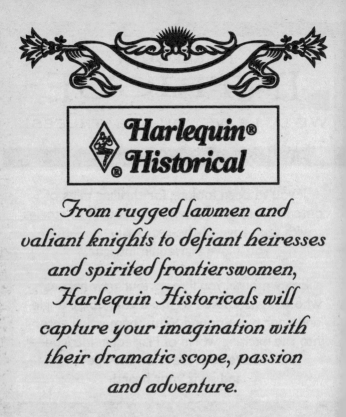

Harlequin® Historical

From rugged lawmen and valiant knights to defiant heiresses and spirited frontierswomen, Harlequin Historicals will capture your imagination with their dramatic scope, passion and adventure.

Harlequin Historicals . . . they're too good to miss!

HHDIR1

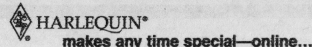